Praise for No

Over the Edge
"McClintock . . . delivers a solid mystery. . . . True McClintock fans will grab a can of pop and gulp down both story and soda in one nervous sitting."
— *Quill & Quire*

Double Cross
"The climax is fraught with danger and emotion, and the conclusion is a satisfying end to a good read."
— *Canadian Materials*

Scared to Death
"Buckle up — it's going to be a scary ride."
— *St. Catharines Standard*

"Lots of suspicious behaviour . . . with a smart, likeable heroine."
— *Canadian Materials*

Hit and Run
"Intensely involving . . . played out with insight and suspense . . . [a] well-crafted mystery."
— *Quill & Quire*

Truth and Lies
"A tautly plotted and suspenseful mystery."
— *Canadian Materials*

SEEING AND BELIEVING

A Mike and Riel Mystery

Norah McClintock

Cover photography by Evan Dion

Scholastic Canada Ltd.

Toronto New York London Auckland Sydney
Mexico City New Delhi Hong Kong Buenos Aires

Scholastic Canada Ltd.
604 King Street West, Toronto, Ontario M5V 1E1, Canada

Scholastic Inc.
557 Broadway, New York, NY 10012, USA

Scholastic Australia Pty Limited
PO Box 579, Gosford, NSW 2250, Australia

Scholastic New Zealand Limited
Private Bag 94407, Greenmount, Auckland, New Zealand

Scholastic Children's Books
Euston House, 24 Eversholt Street, London NW1 1DB, UK

Library and Archives Canada Cataloguing in Publication
McClintock, Norah
Seeing and believing / Norah McClintock.
(A Mike and Riel mystery)
ISBN 0-439-94608-5

I. Title. II. Series: McClintock, Norah Mike and Riel mystery.
PS8575.C62S44 2006   jC813'.54   C2006-900106-5

Photo of the car on the cover by Catherine London

6 5 4 3 2 1   Printed in Canada   06 07 08 09 10

To Joe, Mick and Paul.
Some of it really was true.

CHAPTER ONE

Two plainclothes cops were waiting at the house when Riel and I got back from grocery shopping on Saturday morning. They got out of their you're-not-supposed-to-know-it's-a-cop car as soon as Riel pulled into the driveway. One of them walked over to Riel's side of the car. The other one circled around to my side.

"Are you Michael McGill?" the one on my side said.

I glanced over the roof of the car at Riel.

"Yes, he is," Riel said. "Why?"

"I'm Detective Canton," the cop on Riel's side said. "That's Detective Mancini." Detective Mancini was a lot older than Detective Canton. "And you are?"

"John Riel. I'm responsible for Mike."

Detective Mancini gave Riel a once-over.

"Come here, Mike," Riel said. I wasn't sure why he said it, but I was glad to have a reason to go around the car and stand beside him. Cops make me nervous. Detective Mancini followed close behind me. "What's this about?" Riel said.

Detective Canton focused on me. "Where were you at ten o'clock last night, Mike?" he said.

Riel gave me a "what now?" look.

"I was here."

"Here where? Standing outside in the driveway? Inside the house?"

"Inside the house," I said.

"He's fifteen years old," Riel said. "Why are you asking?"

"Was anyone in the house with you, Mike?" Detective Canton said.

"No," I said. Riel had been out with Susan. My girlfriend, Rebecca, was out of town. Otherwise I would probably have been at her house.

"Did you talk to anyone?" Detective Canton said. "Is there anyone who can confirm you were at home at ten o'clock?"

"No," I said. Geeze, what was going on?

"Why are you asking?" Riel said again. He sounded irritated. He hated having to ask a question more than once. "Are you accusing Mike of something?"

"We're investigating a shooting at a convenience store a few blocks from here," Detective Canton said. "The place was robbed. The man who owns the store was shot. His wife was shot and killed."

Riel half-nodded, which told me that he had heard about it. He kept up with what happened in the neighbourhood.

"You don't think Mike had something to do with that, do you?" he said.

"We're investigating," Detective Canton said. "We're checking to see if anyone in the neighbourhood saw or heard anything." He shifted his eyes back to me. "What were you doing last night, Mike?"

"I was watching TV."

"Yeah? What were you watching?"

What was I watching? He said he was checking to

see if anyone had seen or heard anything, so why was he asking what I'd been watching? "Just stuff. I was clicking around, you know?"

Detective Canton gave me a look like, no, he didn't know, and what's more, it wasn't his job to even begin to know stuff like that about someone like me. I wondered if he had checked me out before he came here to talk to me. If he had, I wondered what picture he had formed in his mind.

"You didn't go out, even for a little while?" he said.

"No."

I glanced at Riel again. Detective Canton had said he was still investigating, but it sounded to me like he thought maybe I was involved. It must have sounded that way to Riel, too, because he said, "If he said he was home, he was home." He sounded even more irritated now.

Detective Canton didn't even look at him. He focused on me.

"So you were inside alone, all night, Mike. Is that right?"

"Not all night," I said. I was getting mad now, too. "John and Susan came home around midnight."

Detective Canton looked to Riel for confirmation of that fact. Riel nodded. The detective's ice-blue eyes came back at me.

"Mike, do you know Vincent Taglia?"

Huh? Where had that question come from? Vin was my best friend — *was* as in, he used to be. I wasn't sure exactly how to describe him now. But I had known him for most of my life, and up until last fall, we had hung out together all the time. Vin and me and our friend Sal. We'd been like a team, until Vin messed everything up.

"Yeah," I said. "I know him."

"When was the last time you saw him?"

I looked at Riel. He nodded, his way of telling me I should answer that one, no problem. He didn't think much of Vin.

"Last fall," I said.

"You haven't seen him since then?"

"No," I said. "Why?" Wait a minute. Did they think Vin had something to do with the convenience store robbery?

"You didn't see him last night? Maybe hang out with him for a while?"

"No."

"Have you seen him today? Has he called you?"

"No."

"Vincent's mother described you as his best friend," Detective Canton said.

I didn't answer.

"But you're saying you haven't seen him in months."

I nodded.

"You haven't seen or talked to your best friend recently?"

"He already told you he hasn't," Riel said.

Detective Canton kept his eyes on me. "Vincent hasn't been home since yesterday. His mother says that's unusual. Do you have any idea where he might go if he needed a place to lay low? Is there someplace special the two of you used to go?"

For sure he thought Vin was involved. Otherwise he wouldn't have asked me that.

"We spent a lot of time at his place," I said. "And at my place — where I used to live, I mean, before I moved in here. Sometimes we used to hang at Sal's place."

"Sal? Do you mean Salvatore San Miguel?"

At first I was surprised by the question. Then I realized that Vin's mother must have given them Sal's name, too. I wondered if they'd talked to him yet.

"Yeah," I said.

"Is there anywhere else you and Vincent hang out?"

Hang out. Present tense. Even I noticed that. He made it sound like Vin and I were together every day, even though I had just told him I hadn't seen Vin in months.

"Just the regular places," I said. "McDonald's, a couple of restaurants near school, an arcade down on Yonge Street."

Detective Canton reached into his pocket and pulled out a card, which he handed to me. "If you see your friend Vincent, or if he contacts you, do yourself a favour, Mike. Call me."

"Do you think Vincent Taglia had something to do with the convenience store robbery?" Riel said.

"We want to talk to him about it," Detective Canton said.

"Vin wouldn't do anything like that," I said. What I really meant was, "He'd never shoot anyone."

"We have a witness who saw three people run out of the store right after gunshots were fired, Mike," Detective Canton said. "The witness identified Vincent Taglia as one of the three. We want to talk to Vincent about that."

"Are you sure it was Vin?" I said. "Maybe the witness got the description wrong. Maybe it was someone who looked like Vin." I turned to Riel. "You're always saying eyewitness evidence is unreliable. You told me that in a lot of the cases where innocent people end up in prison, it's because an eyewitness made a mistake in identifying someone." Riel followed all the big crime stories and trials in the news. He usually had opinions about them, too.

"Are you a lawyer?" Detective Canton asked Riel.

"He's an ex-cop," Detective Mancini said. He seemed to have only one expression: sour. "You must have heard about him. John Riel. Used to be Homicide. His partner got killed."

Riel gave Detective Mancini a sharp look. He handed me his car keys. "Open the trunk, Mike. Let's get the groceries inside."

"We got a positive identification on Vincent Taglia," Detective Canton said. "He was in the store. We want to talk to him. If he contacts you, Mike, call me. Okay?"

"What about the other two people who ran out of the store?" I said.

Detective Canton eyed me suspiciously for a

moment before he said, "We don't know about the other two yet." He kept his eyes on me, watching for a reaction. Then he nodded to Detective Mancini and they walked back to their car.

Where were you at ten o'clock last night, Mike?

What did he think?

Riel watched them go. He nodded at me to go ahead and open the trunk.

"You were home last night, right, Mike?" he said as he reached into the trunk and started handing me plastic bags filled with groceries. But he wasn't looking into the trunk. He was looking into my eyes.

"Yeah, I was home," I said. "All night. You think I would get involved in something like that?"

"No, I don't," Riel said. If he had any doubts, I sure didn't hear them in his voice. That made me feel good.

"I wouldn't lie to you," I said.

"I know."

"There's no way Vin would ever shoot anyone," I said.

Riel grabbed the rest of the groceries and shut the trunk. We walked across the lawn to the porch. The two detectives were still sitting in their car at the curb. I followed Riel inside. We set the groceries on the kitchen table and started putting them away.

"You never talk about him," Riel said.

"What?"

"Vin. You never talk about him."

I shrugged. What was there to talk about? But I thought about him sometimes, and when I did, I usually got mad. He had been in the park one night last fall. He'd kicked a kid when he was down. Afterward, he'd lied about it to take the heat off himself. Sometimes I reminded myself that he had eventually come clean, but the truth was that he'd only done that when he'd run out of other options. Still, in the end, he'd told the cops everything. So had some of the others. And when he was finally charged, it was for assault and obstructing a police investigation, not for murder like three of the guys who were involved. They dropped the second charge when Vin cooperated. He ended up with six months in custody on the assault charge and, from what I'd heard, he was going to testify at the trial when it finally happened. I guess that counted as doing the right thing.

"You haven't seen him at all since he's been out?"

I shook my head. I'd had a hard time believing he'd been involved in what happened to that kid, even though he had been. But robbery and shooting people?

"*You* don't think Vin would do anything like that, do you?" I said to Riel.

Riel shrugged. "They said he was seen running out of the store. If the storeowner identifies him as one of the robbers — "

"If?" I said.

"There was a write-up in the paper this morning. Apparently the storeowner who was shot is in critical condition in hospital. I don't know whether the police got a statement from him or what. I couldn't tell from the paper."

I thought about that as I gathered up all the empty bags and stuffed them into the bag holder under the sink. "I know I'm supposed to clean up my room," I said. Riel insisted I do it every Saturday. "But I have to go out for a little while."

"What for?"

"There's something I need to do."

Riel looked closely at me. "I'm going to ask you one time, Mike, and then I'm not going to ask you again, okay? You told Canton the truth, right? You haven't seen or talked to Vin lately?"

"No, I haven't," I said. "I just — I want to talk to Sal, that's all."

He nodded. He knew that Sal had been tight with Vin and me. And, unlike how he felt about Vin, Riel liked Sal. He kept saying that Sal was a hard worker and that people who worked hard always got somewhere in life.

"Make sure you're home in time to eat something before you go the community centre," he said.

I said I would. I didn't have to start my part-time job at the centre until later.

* * *

Sal was on cash at the McDonald's down near Coxwell. He worked there every weekend and most weeknights in addition to going to school. His father had got sick last fall and had lost his job. Sal said he didn't know when or if his father was going to get better. Sal's mother taught computer skills to new Canadians, but the nonprofit organization she worked for had lost some of its funding, so she was only there part-time now and hadn't been able to find any other job. She'd had to sell their house a few months back and now all three of them — Sal, his father and his mother — were living with Sal's aunt. Sal liked his aunt but hated the cramped quarters and the lack of privacy. He looked tired standing there at the cash, taking orders. He always looked tired these days.

I got in line. When I got to the counter, I said, "You got a break coming up any time soon?"

"In twenty minutes," he said.

"I'll take a Coke," I said. "And I'll wait for you, okay?"

Sal took my money. He scooped ice into a cup and filled it with Coke. He slid it across the counter to me and said, "You want fries with that?" Then he flashed a goofy, just-kidding grin.

Twenty minutes later he came out from behind the counter and nodded for me to follow him outside.

"What's up?" he said.

"The cops were just at Riel's place. They're looking for Vin. They asked me where I was last night."

Sal looked surprised. "Why'd they ask you that?"

"They said it was about a convenience store that was robbed. Two people were shot. One of them died."

"I know," Sal said.

"So they talked to you, too, huh?"

"*I* talked to *them*," Sal said. "Mike, I'm the one who called them."

"What? What do you mean?"

"The store that was robbed is a couple of blocks from here. I was walking by there after my shift last night and I heard this noise — it sounded like a car backfiring or something. Then these two guys came running out. They ran down an alley beside the place."

I stared at him. "And?" I said, even though I wasn't sure I wanted to know.

"I walked toward the store. I was curious, you know. The way those two guys took off, I thought maybe something was going on. Then, *boom,* out comes Vin. He was moving so fast he almost knocked me over. He ran right after the two guys."

I started to get a bad feeling.

"I couldn't figure out what it was all about. Then it hit me — the sound I heard, it wasn't a car backfiring. It was a gun. I went into the store. It was really quiet inside." Sal's eyes had a strange look in them, like he was seeing what he was describing to me. "At first I thought the store was empty. There were candy bars all over the floor in front of the counter where the cash register was, and some shelves had been knocked over. There was stuff all over the floor. Then I saw a woman lying there." He seemed to have to force himself to go on. "She'd been shot in the head, Mike. There was a lot of blood. You wouldn't believe it. I thought I was going to be sick. Then I heard someone groan. It was a man. He was lying on the floor farther back in the store. He'd been shot, too, but in the chest, not the head. He said something about a box — he asked me where the box was. I didn't know what he was talking about. Then he closed his eyes. I thought he was dead. I looked around — there was a phone behind the counter, but I didn't want to go back there. There was so much blood. So I went outside — there's a phone booth right there — and I called 911. The operator said I should stay there until the ambulance and the police got there. She said I shouldn't touch anything and I should make sure no one else went inside the store."

"Geeze."

"Yeah," Sal said. "I couldn't believe it either. When the cops got there, they asked me what I'd seen. So I told them."

"You told them you saw Vin?"

He gave me a look. "What do you think?" He sounded like it was the dumbest question he had ever heard. "Yeah, I told them."

"What about the other two guys? Did you recognize them?"

Sal shook his head. "They were both wearing baggy jeans and big sweatshirts with the hoods pulled up. I didn't see their faces. I couldn't even tell if they were white or black or what. It was dark."

"So how come you could recognize Vin?"

He gave me another look. "I know Vin pretty

well, Mike," he said, talking to me now like I was three years old. "And he wasn't wearing a hoody like the other two guys. At least, I don't think he was. If he was, he didn't have the hood up. Plus he was in the light when I saw him. Anyway, I guess the cops must have showed his picture to the man who was shot, because when I went in this morning to give a formal statement, they said the old man had identified Vin."

"I heard the man was in critical condition."

"Yeah, I heard that, too," Sal said. He shook his head. "Vin really did it this time, huh?"

"You don't really think he was involved, do you?"

Sal looked at me like I was crazy. "Didn't you hear what I just told you, Mike? I saw him. And the old man identified him."

"Did he say Vin was one of the robbers? Or just that he was in the store?"

"He must have said he was one of the robbers. Why else would the cops be looking for him?"

I still couldn't believe it. Vin wasn't perfect. Okay, so he wasn't even close. But to be involved in a shooting? It didn't seem possible.

"How come they asked you where you were last night, Mike?" Sal said.

"I don't know. I guess because Vin and I are friends." Sal gave me a sharp look. "*Were* friends, I mean. His mother told them about me. I guess they were just checking to make sure I wasn't involved."

"You weren't, were you?" Sal said.

"*What?*" What kind of question was that? "Of

course I wasn't. I was at home."

"So Riel backed you up, huh?"

"I'm pretty sure he believes me, but, no, he didn't back me up. He couldn't. He was out with Susan."

"Was Rebecca over?"

I shook my head. "I was home alone."

Sal studied me the same way Detective Canton had.

"Hey, come on, Sal. I was at home. All night."

Sal looked at me for a little longer. Then he checked his watch.

"I have to get back to work," he said.

* * *

When I got home, Riel was on the phone in the living room. He covered the receiver with one hand and said, "I left you some lunch. It's in the fridge." As I went into the kitchen, I heard him say, "No, I haven't told her. I wanted to find out where we stand first. There's no point in upsetting anyone until I know for sure." Who didn't he want to upset? Was he talking about Susan? I got my sandwich out of the fridge and took a big bite, but I stopped chewing again when I heard him say, "Sure, I can be there. But it will have to be after school — after three-thirty." Riel came into the kitchen, the cordless phone wedged between his head and his shoulder, a notepad in one hand, and rooted around in a jar he kept near the fridge for something to write with. He found a pen. He set the pad of paper onto the counter and said, "Give that to me again, Kate."

Who was Kate? Someone from school, maybe

another teacher? But that didn't make sense. If he was going to meet a teacher, he wouldn't have to explain what time school ended.

Riel scribbled something down, and then listened intently to whatever Kate was saying. He was still listening when I finished my sandwich and went to change for work. I had to wave at him to get his attention, and even then I could see I'd only got part of it. Whatever Kate was telling him, it was obviously something important.

"I won't be home tonight until maybe ten," I said. "There's a talent show tonight. I get paid overtime if I stay and clean up afterward."

I spent the next few hours at the community centre, emptying wastepaper baskets and garbage cans, and mopping floors. I checked out the talent show. It was all kids who were taking lessons at the centre — tap, jazz dancing, a little ballet, music, choir. It was okay, but I was glad when it ended. It was dark by the time I'd put the chairs away and mopped the floor. I cut across the park that surrounded the community centre, the same as I always did. I hadn't gone far when someone stepped out from behind a tree. It was Vin.

CHAPTER TWO

"I was beginning to think I'd missed you," Vin said. He smiled at me, but his lips were twitchy and his eyes kept darting around, checking for other people.

"The cops are looking for you," I said.

Vin nodded and stepped back into the shadow of the tree.

"Did they talk to you?"

"They asked me if I'd seen you or if I knew where you were. They also asked me where I was at ten o'clock last night."

"You?" Vin said. "Why'd they ask you that?"

"Your mother told them I was your friend. I guess they're checking with people you know."

"Did they talk to Sal?"

I could think of only one reason why he was asking that question. But I still couldn't believe it.

"Yeah, they talked to him. So did I. He says he saw you run out of the store. He also says the man that was shot identified you."

Vin's shoulders slumped. "I didn't do anything, Mike," he said. "Honest."

"I think the cops have a different idea. And Sal *saw* you."

"I was there," Vin said. "I was in the store when it happened. But I didn't have anything to do with it. I swear it, Mike. This time, I wasn't involved."

This time.

I wished it wasn't dark. That way I'd have been able to get a better look at Vin's face.

"So you saw what happened, right?" I said.

"Yeah. I saw it."

"Then all you have to do is go to the cops and tell them."

"I don't know," Vin said. "I wish it was that simple."

I started to get a bad feeling again.

"What do you mean?"

"I mean, it's not like I can tell them who did it or anything. It was two guys, but I don't know who they are. They came into the store after me and they were wearing big hooded sweatshirts, just plain navy blue, and big jeans. I couldn't see their faces or anything."

"So tell the cops that."

"I thought it would be better to wait," he said.

"Wait for what?"

"What if they don't believe me?"

"But if it's the truth — "

"Come on, Mike. After what happened with Robbie, they're going to assume I was involved."

"But you weren't, right, Vin?" I didn't feel the least bit bad asking him that after he'd already told me he wasn't. I wanted him to say it over and over again, and I wanted him to look me in the eye every time he said it.

"Geeze, no, Mike. What kind of person do you think I am?"

That was the problem. I wasn't sure anymore.

"You have to believe me, Mike. I was in the wrong place at the wrong time. That's all. I was on my way home. I got thirsty. And I went into that store to get a Coke. Boy, do I ever wish I went somewhere else instead or just waited until I got home. But I didn't." He shook his head. "I can still see it, Mike. I go into the store and I guess these two guys come in behind me. But I don't pay any attention to them. Why should I? All I want is a Coke. So I go over to the coolers. They're along one wall, near the back of the store. Then I just happen to look up and these two guys are there. They're up at the front near the cash register, and there's a woman behind the counter. One of the guys is looking at the candy bars — they're displayed all along the bottom of the counter, you know how they are in most places, right, Mike?"

I could picture it. Most of those stores are laid out in the same way and they always have the gum and the candy bars up near the cash, I think mostly so they can watch that kids don't steal them.

"I'm digging a Coke out of the cooler and I turn around and I see one of the guys holding something in his hand. It was a gun, Mike. I couldn't believe it. I'm standing there and I'm thinking, this has to be a joke. This can't be real. I mean, it's like something out of a bad movie. But it *was* real. The guy had a gun and he's telling the woman to hand over all the cash. And I just freeze. I felt like I couldn't even breathe. You know that feeling, Mike?"

Boy, did I ever.

I heard something jingle behind me and turned and saw a man walking a dog on a leash a couple of metres away. He peered at us through the darkness. Vin stepped deeper into the shadows. He waited until the man and the dog were long gone before he continued.

"So the woman starts to come out from behind the counter. She has money in her hands and she's holding it out to the guy, and he's yelling at her to stay where she is, just stay there and give him the money," he said. "But she keeps coming toward him with her hands out, holding the money. And I'm thinking, Just take the money and go. Get out of here. And then I don't know what happened. The woman is still holding out the money in her hand and the gun goes off. I don't know if the guy meant to shoot her or what. But, anyway, the gun goes off and the guy grabs the money out of the woman's hand as she's going down. You ever seen anyone get shot, Mike?" What a question. Of course I hadn't. "It's not what you expect, Mike. There was blood all over the place." Sal had said the same thing. "And the sounds — I heard her hit the ground, Mike. Then this old man comes in from I don't even know where and all of a sudden he starts to yell and they shoot him, too. Then they take off. I look at the old guy who's on the floor, and he looks at me, and, geeze, Mike, I didn't even know what I was doing, I just take off, too, you know? I don't even remember it that clearly. I know I knocked over a whole bunch of stuff on my way out. I got out of the store and

19

took off around a corner. That's when I see that the two guys have run around the same corner and they're still running. So I turn and run the other way. I kept running, Mike, until I was ready to fall down from running so much."

Running had been stupid.

"The cops said the woman died and the old guy's in critical condition," I said.

"Yeah, I heard," Vin said. "But he managed to identify me first, right? That's what Sal said, right?" I nodded. "Talk about bad luck," Vin said.

"The guy's critical, Vin. That means he could die."

"Yeah, but I didn't do it. I wasn't involved." I could hardly see Vin, he was so deep in the shadows between a couple of big trees. "So I thought I'd wait and see."

"Wait and see about *what?*" I said. It was the second time he'd mentioned waiting.

"Did the cops or Sal say anything to you about the girl?"

"What girl?"

"They didn't mention her?"

"What girl, Vin?"

"There was a girl in the store."

I shook my head. "Sal said there were two people in the store — the woman lying behind the counter and the old man lying farther back in the store," I said. "He didn't say anything about a girl."

"She was there, Mike. In the back. I saw her. She had short spiky black hair, and a ring in her eyebrow, and a spider tattoo on her arm, right here."

He touched the outside of his upper left arm. "I don't know what she was doing back there, but I saw her. I'm pretty sure those two guys didn't, but I did. I saw her back there. That girl can tell the cops I wasn't involved, Mike. Are you sure they didn't mention her?"

"Nobody said anything to me about a girl," I said. "But cops never say much to regular people. They didn't even tell me it was Sal who saw you. I found out from him."

"I thought it'd be best to wait, you know, until the cops talk to that girl. It could save me a lot of hassle if that girl tells them I didn't come in with those guys and that I wasn't anywhere near the cash when it happened."

Now I was confused. "You could have told them that yourself, Vin. Running away was bad enough. But hiding out like this — that's stupid." I couldn't help wondering how come Sal hadn't mentioned seeing a girl. I wished again that it wasn't so dark, so I could get a good look at Vin. Maybe then I'd be able to tell if he was snowing me, trying out a story on me that he was maybe going to try out on the cops next. But how smart was that? Then again, how smart was Vin? "If there was a girl, she would have gone to the cops by now," I said. "You've got nothing to worry about, right?"

"I was just waiting to hear something about it — like the cops have a witness and they're looking for those two guys. Two, Mike, not three. Not me," Vin said. "Because otherwise, all they've got to go on is

Sal seeing me do maybe the stupidest thing I ever did and the old guy identifying me as being there. Which means they're going to arrest me. Probable cause, right? You don't know what it's like, Mike. I mean, unless that girl has told it and told it right, they're going to lock me up. With that woman dead, there's no way they're going to let me walk around until there's a trial. Because that's what's going to happen next. And it can take time. They haven't even had the trial for Robbie yet. Being in custody is awful, Mike. You can't do what you want when you want. You can't even go home. And some of the kids I was in with that time, they were really messed up. I don't want to go through that again, you know?"

"I know," I said. "But the cops are looking for you. Sooner or later they're going to find you."

"I'm scared, Mike."

I tried to imagine myself in his position. I felt sorry for him.

"We could go back to Riel's place. He'll know what to do," I said.

Vin shifted back into the shadows. "I don't know."

"Vin, you don't have any choice."

"Riel will probably slap the cuffs on me himself."

"He's not what you think, Vin," I said. Sure, Riel was strict. He insisted that homework came first. He insisted I hold down a job, but that it not interfere with my schoolwork. He insisted I learn to cook. He insisted that I keep my room clean and that I do my share of the chores around the house.

But he was fair and I trusted him. "Come on. Let's go."

Vin stepped out of the shadows. He nodded and moved closer to the path that cut through the park. When he stepped into a puddle of light under a lamppost, I saw how terrible he looked, like he hadn't slept in a long time. He had probably been awake since it had happened, and that was nearly twenty-four hours ago now. His face was dirty, too. I wondered where he'd been all day. We started down the path toward the road.

We were on Riel's street, almost at his house, when a cop car slid past us. Vin froze, which was the wrong thing to do. If one of those cops checked his rearview or sideview mirror and saw Vin tense up like that, he'd be suspicious. He'd be doubly suspicious if he had Vin's description.

The cop car slowed. I glanced at Vin. His eyes were focused on the cop car, and it looked to me like he was getting ready to run. I grabbed his arm. The cop car had reversed and was backing toward us. Vin tried to pull away, but I held him, afraid of what could happen if he bolted. Two cops jumped out of the car, one on each side. They had their guns out and they were pointing them at us.

"Put your hands above your head," one of them said. My hands shot up. Vin shrunk into a crouch, like he was going into a starter's pose. "Vincent Taglia?" the cop said. Vin nodded, but just barely. I saw Riel out of the corner of my eye. He came out of the house and jogged over to the cops, but stood back and didn't say anything right away.

"Vincent Taglia, you're under arrest," the cop said. He took Vin by the arm and led him over to the police car. He told Vin what he was being arrested for. Then he told him his rights and asked him if he understood what each of the rights meant. Vin said he did. The cop made Vin put his hands on the car, and he patted Vin down. Then he made him turn out his pockets. Vin didn't have much in there — some gum, some matches, a couple of what looked like five-dollar bills. The cop looked carefully at those. Then he shone a flashlight down the front of Vin's clothes — his jacket and his sweatshirt and his jeans. He kept the flashlight on the bottom of Vin's jeans for a few moments. He said, "What's that mark on your pants? Is that blood, Vincent?"

"Geeze, no," Vin said.

"Vin, you don't have to answer any questions," Riel said. Vin turned to look at him, surprised. "If you say anything, they can use it. You should wait until you've talked to a lawyer. Minimum, you should wait until you've contacted your parents."

The cop glanced at Riel, then he turned his flashlight on the bills Vin had pulled from his pocket.

"Where did you get these?" he asked.

"I don't know. The bank machine. Where else do you get money?"

"Vin — " Riel cautioned.

"You don't get five-dollar bills from a bank machine, Vincent," the cop said. He peered at the bills again. "What's this on these bills, Vincent?" he said.

Vin shrugged.

"Looks like dried blood," the cop said. "Is that what that is?"

I stared at Vin.

"If we get that analyzed, are we going to find out that there's blood on your jeans and blood on this money and that it belongs to the woman you shot in that store?"

"Geeze, no," Vin said. "I mean, maybe it's blood. I don't know. Look, I was in the store, okay?" Riel shook his head in disgust. "But I didn't do anything. I sure didn't shoot anyone. I saw that money lying in the alley after I left the store. It was just lying there, so I picked it up. But I figured if I told you that . . . " His voice trailed off. He looked at me the way a dog looks at you when you're about to leave the house, but you're not holding a leash in your hand. "Hey, Mike," he said. "You ever seen me pass up free money?"

I didn't know what to say.

The cop handcuffed Vin and put him in the back of the police car.

Then they got around to me. When they asked me for my name, I told them. Then Riel stepped forward and identified himself.

"We were coming home," I said to Riel. "Vin was going to talk to the cops. It's all a big mistake. He was scared, so we were coming home and we were going to get you to call the cops for him."

Riel told the two cops that I was fifteen. He asked them if they suspected me of any wrongdoing. I held my breath as I waited for the answer. They said no, but they wanted to know why I was with Vin, who was wanted because of a murder-robbery at a convenience store. Riel told me I should answer all their questions. They had about a million of them. Finally they said they wanted me to go down to the police station the next day to make a formal statement.

"But I don't know anything," I said.

"They just want you to say again what you've said and it'll be written down," Riel said. He promised them that I'd be there.

* * *

"You want to tell me how you managed to find Vin when the police couldn't?" Riel said after the cops had left.

"It's like I already told the cops." He gave me a sharp look now that we were alone. *"Police,"* I said, correcting myself. Riel is one of those people who doesn't like the word *cop*. He says it's disrespectful and insists that I say police or police officer instead. I don't see what the big deal is. I've met a couple of his cop friends and they don't make a big deal about it. One of them, a homicide detective named Jones, always refers to himself as a cop. "I didn't find Vin. He found me. He was waiting outside the community centre when I got off work."

Riel stared at me for so long it scared me. Finally

he said, "I thought you said you haven't seen him since last fall."

"I haven't." Geeze, what was his problem?

"So how did he know where to find you?" Riel said. "How did he even know you were working at the community centre?"

"I don't know." Riel looked hard at me. "Maybe he asked someone," I said. "A lot of people know I work there."

"So when the police were here this morning and asked you if you'd seen Vin or knew where he might be and you said no, you were telling them the truth, right, Mike?"

"Yeah." Did he think I'd be stupid enough to lie to him after everything I'd been through last year? "Tonight was the first time I've seen Vin since last fall. He was waiting for me in the park when I got off work. He told me what happened. He says he was in the wrong place at the wrong time. He wasn't with the guys who robbed the store. But he was in the store when they came in. He says that they shot the woman and then the old man came in and they shot him. Vin says he was scared. If it was me, I'd have been scared, too. So he ran. He says he knows it was stupid, but he wasn't thinking. He says there was a girl in the store that the two guys didn't see. He says she can back him up. He's pretty sure she saw everything and that she can tell the police that he had nothing to do with it."

Riel looked at me for a few moments before he

said, "If Vin sticks with that story, he's going to be in for a rough ride."

"What do you mean, *if* he sticks with that story? He swears that's what happened."

Riel shook his head. "Think about it, Mike. The two guys shoot the woman. Then, according to Vin, the old man shows up and they shoot him. But they don't do anything to Vin, who's a witness to the robbery and shooting? Does *that* make any sense to you?"

"Maybe they figured someone must have heard the shots and had already called the cops. Maybe they panicked. Vin said they got out of there pretty fast after they shot the old man."

Riel didn't look even remotely convinced. He said, "But instead of going to the police and telling them what he saw, like a good citizen" — like Sal, I thought — "Vin hides out for nearly twenty-four hours. Then, when the police finally find him, he's got some money in his pocket that probably came from the store. And when the police ask him about it, first he says he doesn't know where he got the money. Then he changes his story and says the robbers dropped it in an alley and he picked it up. Does that make any sense? He's so scared that he runs away from the scene instead of staying and calling for help, but when he sees money lying in the alley, he stops to pick it up?"

"When you say it like that — "

"I'm not the one who said it, Mike. That's what Vin said. And then he tells you there was a girl in the store, someone who saw the whole thing." His tone of voice — a real teacher tone — told me he didn't believe it. "What did Sal say? What did he see?" He surprised me when he said that. The cops who had come to the house that morning had mentioned Sal, but they hadn't said he was a witness.

"You know about Sal?" I said.

"His mother called me. She's worried something could happen to Sal because he spoke to the police. Where she comes from, the authorities weren't always the good guys."

I knew that. Sal had told me all about life in Guatemala.

"Did Sal say anything to you about seeing a girl, Mike?"

I shook my head. "He said he didn't see anyone except the woman and the old man. Maybe the girl ran, too."

"Right," Riel said. "Just like Vin. Everybody runs. Nobody calls the police. Nobody comes forward to say what happened. If I were on this case, Mike, I wouldn't buy it. Not any of it. Not for one minute."

"What do you think is going to happen?"

"That's going to depend on Vin."

CHAPTER THREE

It was in the paper that I found on the kitchen table the next morning: *Police make arrest in convenience store shooting*. It was one of those small stories, the kind that runs in a column down one side of the page, each story only a paragraph, some of the stories hardly any longer than the headline. It didn't mention Vin by name. It called him "a youth, age sixteen, who cannot be named under the Youth Criminal Justice Act." It said the police had evidence. It didn't say what it was, but I already knew.

I heard a rustling sound behind me and caught a whiff of perfume. Susan.

"Hey, Mike," she said, her voice bright like she had a smile in it. She was wearing a robe over a sleeveless T-shirt and pyjama bottoms. She didn't have any make-up on yet, but she looked terrific. She always did. "You working today?" she said.

I nodded. "Noon to six." I worked every Saturday, every other Sunday, and a couple of times a week, depending on when they had events they needed me to set up for and clean up after. "You?"

"I've got the evening shift today and tomorrow," she said. "Then I'm off for three days." Susan was a doctor. She worked in the emergency room at the hospital that was just a couple of blocks from Riel's house. "I'm going to be glad when school's out for the summer. Then maybe when I have a day off, John will be around."

"You guys really should go somewhere," I said. "After the wedding, I mean." Riel and Susan were getting married at the end of June — six weeks from now — but had decided not to take a honeymoon right away.

"We'll get around to it," Susan said, real casual about it, like it was no big deal. I didn't believe it, though. The way I heard it, all brides were dying to go somewhere special after their wedding. "It'll be nice to have John off all summer. We can really get organized."

Susan was going to move in with us. Into Riel's house, I mean.

"Yeah, but don't you two want some time alone?" I said. Riel had never come out and said it, but I was pretty sure that I was the reason they weren't going on a honeymoon, that Riel didn't know what to do with me if he went away for a couple of weeks. "I can look after myself, you know."

Susan smiled and poured herself some coffee.

"I know you can, Mike," she said. "We'll get away eventually. Just not this summer." She glanced at the newspaper. "Are you finished with that?"

I folded it and handed it to her. She tucked it under her arm and started out of the kitchen with it and her coffee.

"Is he still here?" I said. Ever since Riel had proposed to Susan, she had started staying over. Not all of the time, but more and more often. I still hadn't got totally used to it. I didn't mind that she was here so much. Susan was easy to be around and mostly — so far — she left it up to Riel to deal with me. He was my foster parent, not her. She never told me what to do and never yelled at me when I didn't do something I was supposed to. It was like good cop (Susan, who was fun and liked to laugh) and bad cop (Riel, who was stern and strict). No, the thing about having Susan in the house, the thing that I couldn't quite believe even when I saw it right there in front of me, was the way Riel acted. It wasn't like he turned to mush with Susan or anything, but his face lit up when she walked into the room and he smiled a whole lot more when she was around. He relaxed more, too.

"He went out for a run," Susan said. "He said he'd be back in time to go to the police station with you before you go to work." She headed for the stairs.

"Oh, hey, Susan?" I called to her. "Wait a minute."

She turned. I brushed past her — boy, she smelled great — into the living room, and grabbed a videocassette from the shelf under the TV.

"This is for you," I said, handing the cassette to her.

She turned it over, looking for a label, but there wasn't one.

"What's this?" she said.

"It's a surprise."

She examined it again.

"Give me a hint," she said.

I shook my head. A surprise is a surprise.

"You're a real man of mystery, Mike." She smiled at me, tucked the cassette under her arm with the newspaper, and went upstairs.

Riel was back at ten-thirty to drive me to the police station. He came in with me and sat there while I talked to one of the cops who had arrested Vin. The cop asked me over and over how I had found Vin, and I told him over and over that I hadn't found Vin, he had found me. When he asked me what Vin had said, I told him what Vin had told me — that he hadn't been involved in the robbery and the shooting. I told him what Vin had said about the girl, too. The cop didn't say anything. He'd probably already heard it from Vin. He didn't ask me again where I had been the night of the robbery, and I was relieved at that. He wrote down what I said, read it back to me, asked me if I wanted to add or change anything, and then made me sign it.

After we finished at the police station, Riel drove me to work. Maybe ten or fifteen times that day, pretty much every time I passed one of the pay phones in the community centre, I thought about calling Vin's house to see how his mom and dad were doing. For a while back when we were kids, I'd spent almost as much time at Vin's house as I had at my own. His parents used to call me "the other son we never had." But every time I looked at the phone, I imagined Vin's mom or his dad picking up at the other end, and then I imagined myself fumbling for something to say, stammering and stuttering and in the end saying . . . what? *I'm sorry to hear that Vin got arrested? I'm sorry Vin was in the wrong place at the wrong time* (if you believe what he said) or *I'm sorry he messed up even worse this time* (if you believe what the cops were saying and what Sal and Riel thought). Either way, it wouldn't make them feel any better.

And what about me? What did I think?

I hated to admit it, but what Riel said made a lot of sense. Why would the guys who robbed the store shoot the woman and the man, but do nothing to Vin, an eyewitness to the whole thing? Maybe it was like Vin said, maybe they had panicked and run. Vin had said that he couldn't identify the two guys. Maybe that explained why they hadn't done anything to him. But how would they have known that? How could they have been sure that he hadn't seen their faces or that there wasn't something, even something small, that Vin could tell the police about them?

And then there was the thing about the money. First he'd told the cops who arrested him that he didn't know where he got the money, that it must have come from a bank machine. Then, as soon as one of the cops mentioned blood on the money, Vin said he'd picked it up in the alley when he was running away. He was scared, he was running, but he stopped to pick up money. I tried to decide if that was something I would have done.

On the other hand, according to Vin, the other two guys had their faces hidden by hoods. Vin didn't. That's why the storeowner was able to identify him, but not the other two. It was also why Sal had been able to identify him. What kind of person goes to rob a store with two other guys and doesn't even bother to try to cover his face, especially when the other two guys who are involved cover *their* faces? I mean, you'd have to be pretty stupid, right?

And then there was the girl. Vin had said there was a girl in the back of the store. He was pretty sure she had seen the whole thing and could tell the cops that he wasn't involved. Well, the cops had arrested Vin, which meant they didn't just *think* he was involved, they were pretty sure of it. So obviously that girl hadn't come forward. Or if she had come forward, she hadn't backed Vin up. Instead of saying something that could clear him, she must have incriminated him, which meant that he had been mistaken about what the girl would say. And *that* meant that either he really was involved, or the girl thought he was. So why would he make a big deal about her being able to clear him?

Maybe it was like Riel thought — there was no girl. She didn't exist. Vin was making her up. Sal hadn't seen a girl. The cops hadn't mentioned a girl (but then the cops didn't talk about all the details of anything, ever). Still, why would Vin say there was a girl in the store who could tell the cops he wasn't involved if there was no girl? How would that help him? It wouldn't. It just plain wouldn't. Even Vin would see that.

It didn't make sense. None of it did.

Unless Vin was telling the truth.

Maybe Vin's face wasn't hidden because he really wasn't involved. Maybe he ran because he really was scared. Maybe he had really picked up the money without thinking, just because it was there. And maybe it was there because the guys who had robbed the store really had dropped it.

And maybe the girl really existed.

Maybe she had seen what had happened and could help Vin out. But for some reason she hadn't come forward. But why hadn't she? If I'd been in her position, I'd be talking to the police for sure. If she wasn't talking, what did that mean? That didn't make any sense either.

It was giving me a headache just thinking about it . . .

The likeliest thing was that Vin had flat-out lied to me. He'd done it before. Maybe it had turned into a habit.

And, let's face it, if I had been in that store to rob it, wouldn't I say I didn't do it? I mean, who's stupid enough right away to say, Yeah, I was involved in a shooting where someone got killed and someone else ended up in the hospital? Especially if the other guys who did it got away? Nobody, that's who. Not even Vin.

* * *

Riel was in the living room reading when I got home. He reads a lot. Mostly history. Mostly, I think, so he'll know what he's talking about when he stands up in front of the class. He glanced up when I came in.

"How was work?"

"Okay."

"You hungry? I made some chili."

The one thing my uncle Billy used to know how to make was chili, but his was mostly meat, beans and tomatoes. Riel makes vegetarian chili — beans and peppers, onions, mushrooms, corn, tomatoes, all very spicy. It's okay. But would it kill him to stir in a little hamburger?

"Sounds good," I said. "I'll heat some up."

"How about your homework? Is that done?"

"I'm working on it."

He glanced at his watch. His point: it was getting late.

"Don't worry," I said. "I don't have much to do."

"Exams are coming up soon."

"I know." Geeze, I knew he meant well, but he could relax once in a while. I hesitated. "If I wanted to see Vin, how would I go about doing that?"

Riel looked at me, surprised. "*Do* you want to see him?"

"I don't know," I said. "I was just wondering." No, that wasn't true. The truth was: "Yeah, I do."

"Mind if I ask why?" He had that look on his face — it's just a question, it's no big deal. But I knew it was more than that.

I shrugged. "I've known him forever."

Riel waited.

"I know you think he's pretty messed up. But — " But what? "But I *have* known him forever. And . . . I want to talk to him. I need to look at him and see if he's lying to me. Maybe that doesn't make sense, but I need to know."

Riel looked at me for a few moments before he said, "I'll see what I can do."

CHAPTER FOUR

Considering that Vin's name hadn't been in the paper, a whole lot of people at school seemed to know that he was the one who'd been arrested. There was only one person I could think of who could have spread the word. Sal.

"I can't believe he told everyone," I said to Rebecca at lunchtime. Rebecca has thick coppery-red hair, dark brown eyes, a ton of freckles and a beautiful smile. She makes me feel like the luckiest guy in the world.

"I can't believe *you* didn't tell *me*," she said. "I mean, someone you know gets arrested right in front of your house, and you didn't even call me. How come?"

I shrugged. The truth was, I had been so wrapped up in what had happened that it hadn't occurred to me to call her. But I sure didn't want to tell her that. She might take it the wrong way, like I thought she wasn't important.

"You were at that thing for your grandparents," I said. Rebecca had been up at her grandparents' place in Muskoka all weekend. They'd been celebrating some milestone anniversary.

"Yeah, but I had my cell," she said. "You could have called me."

"Sorry," I said. But I was still thinking about Sal. "He should have kept his mouth shut," I said. "I mean, the media isn't allowed to report Vin's name.

So why is it okay for Sal to broadcast it?"

"Well, he's not the media," Rebecca said. She studied me for a moment. "Why are you so mad at him anyway?"

"He's the one who identified Vin to the cops."

She looked surprised. "If you'd been standing outside that store and you heard shooting and then saw someone run out of the store and you recognized that person, wouldn't you have told the cops?"

I knew the correct answer was, Yes, you bet. Maybe I would have said it, too, if the someone she was talking about wasn't someone who'd spent most of his life as my best friend.

"You would, wouldn't you, Mike? I mean, even if it was me, you'd tell them, right?"

"You'd never do anything like that," I said. I smiled at her, trying to keep it light.

She put down her sandwich. "You're walking by a convenience store late at night. You hear gunshots. You see me run out of the store and down an alley — " Geeze, it sounded like Sal hadn't held back on any details. " — and then you go into the store and you see that two people, two actual people, have been shot. Are you telling me you wouldn't say, Hey, I know who did it, I can give you her name and tell you where she lives? Is *that* what you're telling me?"

"Come on, Rebecca."

"I mean, Sal saw what he saw."

Rebecca had transferred to my school last fall. All

she knew about Vin was the trouble he had been in around that time and how he'd tried to lay it off on me. But she actually knew Sal. She liked him. And during the time that she'd known him, Sal hadn't been in any trouble.

"Rebecca, you don't understand." It was the wrong thing to say. She started to re-wrap her sandwich. "Hey," I said, reaching for her hand. She yanked it away from me and stuffed her sandwich into her backpack. Then she got up and started threading her way through the crowded tables toward the cafeteria door. I got up to follow her. That's when I saw Riel coming toward me.

"Trouble?" he said, nodding at Rebecca, who was getting smaller and smaller the closer she got to the cafeteria door. I shrugged. Riel looked at me, like he was trying to figure out what was going on. He said, "If you want to see Vin this afternoon, I'll run you out there."

"Really?" I said. "Are you sure you want to?"

"No, I'm not. But if it's what you want, I'll do it. Meet me in the parking garage right after school, okay?"

* * *

I ran into Sal after school when I was on my way to meet Riel. He was at his locker, packing textbooks and binders into his backpack.

"Hey," I said. "Did you have to tell everyone?"

"Tell everyone what?" he said. He sounded confused.

"About Vin. You told everyone about Vin."

"No, I didn't. I only told Imogen," he said. "That's all."

"Imogen?" I knew only one person named Imogen. "You mean Imogen from my French class?" He nodded. "Why would you tell her?"

Sal's cheeks turned red. What was going on? What was I missing?

Wait a minute. "Are you and Imogen . . . you know?"

"I like her, okay?" Sal said, like he was daring me to tell him no, it's not okay. "She's nice. We get along."

I stared at him. I thought I knew Sal pretty well. He'd hung out with Vin and me for years. Of the three of us, Sal had always been the most serious, the straightest arrow. He was also the quietest one and shy around girls. Not that he was perfect. Sal had had his share of scrapes. He'd raided a bakery truck with Vin and me one night, ripping off some boxes of cake. But that seemed like a whole lifetime ago now. Sal had changed since then. A lot of it had to do with his dad being sick. Sal was helping to support his family, which meant he had to work twice as hard as me, and that had made him seem a decade older almost overnight. Now there was a girl in his life and I hadn't even noticed. He hadn't told me, either.

"The thing is, Sal, when you tell something like that to one person around here, you might as well go down to the office, turn on the microphone on Gianneris's desk and announce it to the whole school."

Sal jammed a textbook into his backpack and slammed his locker shut. "You don't talk to Rebecca?" he said. "You don't tell her when something happens to you?"

"Yeah, I talk to her."

"That's all I did, Mike. I talked to Imogen about something that happened to me."

"You talked to her about something that happened to *Vin*," I said. "And because of that, everyone thinks that Vin was involved in shooting those people. You know how it's supposed to work, Sal. Innocent until proven guilty. *Proven.*"

Sal threaded his lock into the catch on his locker door. "I don't care about Vin," he said. "I stopped caring about Vin a long time ago. And when I talked to Imogen, it wasn't about Vin. It was about me. I went in that store, and I saw that woman lying there in all that blood. Her eyes were open, Mike. She was staring up, but she wasn't really staring because she couldn't see anything anymore. There was a hole in the middle of her face. And there was stuff in the blood. Pieces of stuff that, I don't know, I sure didn't ask, but I watch TV the same as everyone else, so I started imagining what it was, and now I can't stop thinking about it." He sounded mad now and his voice was loud. "I thought I was going to be sick or faint or something. I think the only reason I didn't was I heard that man groaning. He was still breathing and he needed help, and that got me through it. I helped him. I made a phone call and then I did everything that you're supposed to do, you know, everything they tell you to do. *That's* what I talked to Imogen about — because who else am I going to talk to about that? You?"

"What's that supposed to mean? Why wouldn't you talk to me about it?"

"Right," he said. "Look at the way you're acting. Look at the way you acted right from the start. Like you can't believe Vin would do anything like this. Even when I tell you what I saw, you don't believe it. When you came to talk to me on Saturday, you made it pretty clear that you think *I'm* the one who made a mistake, not Vin. First you think I saw it wrong, and now you think I did something wrong."

"I never said — "

"I know he's your best friend, Mike. I know it, okay? I was always the third wheel on a two-wheel bike — okay to hang around with, okay to mess up with, okay to help you out lately when Vin's been gone, but not the same as Vin, right? Not as good as him. I always thought that and now I see I was right."

"Geeze, Sal — "

"I know what I saw, Mike. And I know I did the right thing. So if I want to talk to Imogen or anyone else about it, it's none of your business." He yanked the pull cord on his backpack and slung one of the straps over his shoulder. "I have to get to work."

I watched him stride down the hall, taking big,

angry steps, like he couldn't get away from me fast enough. I felt like I was watching a stranger.

* * *

Riel was standing next to his car, drumming his fingers on the roof, when I got to the underground parking. He made a point of looking at his watch when he saw me coming.

"I said right after school, Mike."

"I'm sorry," I said.

"Because I'm doing you a favour. You know that, right?"

"Yeah, I know." I yanked open the passenger door and got inside. Riel climbed in behind the wheel. He glanced at me. I thought he was going to say something, but he just turned the key in the ignition. We were out of the parking garage, down the street and onto the expressway before he said, "I just want to make sure you don't get hurt."

"Hurt?" I looked at him. "How am I going to get hurt?"

Riel flicked on the left-turn signal and changed lanes to pass a truck. He didn't answer until he'd settled back into the middle lane.

"When I decided to try for the police college, a friend of mine — a good friend — decided to try it, too. We both got in. We went through together. We got hired together. We hung out together. We got promoted together. Then I went into Traffic." Accident investigation, he meant. "He went into the drug squad."

I hadn't heard this story. Riel wasn't big on

spilling the details of his life. But I would have bet everything I had in the bank, which by now actually amounted to something, that I knew where the story was going.

"I thought the drug squad didn't exist anymore," I said.

Riel looked at me, like he was wondering how I knew that. Billy had told me. He'd said a lot of the cops in it turned out to be corrupt, so it had been disbanded. Billy thought that was funny. He never did have a high opinion of cops.

"This is from before," Riel said. "Maybe five years ago. I started to hear rumours — my friend was getting tight with the wrong people, he was looking the other way, he was taking money, that kind of thing. But I didn't want to believe them — because he was my friend."

Yeah, if I'd bet, I'd have made a bundle.

"Rumours?" I said. "I thought you didn't listen to rumours." I thought he didn't believe in them.

"At first I didn't. But I kept hearing them. So I decided to ask him if they were true."

"And?"

"He looked me in the eye and told me that they weren't. And I believed him."

"But it turned out they were true, right?" I said. Why else would he be telling me this story?

"He swore to me that he didn't do anything wrong. He told me it was all a mistake, that it wasn't what they were saying it was. But they showed me what they had on him, Mike. I saw the proof."

"But up until then, you believed him, right?" I said. "You gave him the benefit of the doubt. Right?"

It took a couple of seconds before Riel nodded.

"That's all I want to do," I said. "I want to give Vin the benefit of the doubt."

"There isn't much doubt in Vin's case," Riel said. I knew that was what he thought. It was probably what everyone thought. "And sometimes — a lot of times — when people screw up, they try to cover it up. They lie — even to their friends." Like Riel's friend had lied to him.

I believed Riel when he said he didn't want me to get hurt. But there was something he was forgetting.

"You don't know Vin," I said. "I do."

Riel didn't say anything. We drove the rest of the way in silence.

* * *

They had Vin locked up. Riel and I both had to show ID. Riel said he'd called ahead. He said who he'd talked to. We had to sign in. They asked us if we had any packages for Vin, but we didn't. Then we had to wait around for a while before they let me into what they called the visiting room. It was a large, plain room with cement-block walls and lots of tables and chairs that were all bolted to the floor. After I sat down, a door opened and Vin was shown in. He had looked bad the last time I saw him. He didn't look any better now. I wondered what it was like in here, what kind of room he had, whether he had a roommate or was on his own, whether people hassled him or left him alone. We sat down at one of the tables. The whole time we were talking, a man watched us.

"Is he listening to what we're saying?" I said.

Vin shook his head. "He just wants to make sure nothing happens, that's all. They have all kinds of rules here, Mike. You think Riel's tough? Man, he's like a vacation compared to this place." He was smiling, though, and seemed glad that I was there. "I was real surprised when they told me you were coming to see me. You never came to see me last time." I couldn't make myself look at him when he said that. Instead, I focused on the tabletop. "It's okay, though," he said. "I understand. I mean, if it had been the other way around, I would have been pretty mad at you. I don't think I'd have come to visit you, either. But when I saw you the other day — I don't want to sound weird or anything, but it made me feel good, you know?"

"Yeah," I said. Despite everything, I'd felt the same way. I looked up at him. "I wish things were different, though."

"Tell me about it."

"Vin, did you tell the cops about the girl?"

He snorted. "Yeah, I told them. One of them wrote it down. But the next time they talked to me, the same guy that wrote it down told me my imaginary girlfriend wasn't going to save me. That's what he called her, Mike. My imaginary girlfriend. Like I made her up."

"But you didn't, right?" I said.

Vin gave me a sharp look, as if I'd insulted him. But instead of getting mad, he just shook his head. "I really messed up good if it's got to the point where my oldest friend has to ask me a question like that."

Oldest friend. Not best friend. I wondered how much he'd thought about those words before he said them. I mumbled that I was sorry, but Vin shook his head again.

"You've got nothing to be sorry about, Mikey. You had nothing to do with it."

I glanced at the big clock on the wall. Riel had told me I had fifteen minutes.

"The cops are acting like they don't know anything about the girl," Vin said. "They think I'm spinning them a story, which means that she hasn't come forward. She hasn't gone to the cops and told them what she saw. Why do you think that is, Mike?"

Why did I think she hadn't come forward? Maybe because Vin *was* spinning a story. But what would he gain by it?

"Maybe she's scared," Vin said. "It's the only thing I can think of. Maybe she thinks something will happen to her if she goes to the cops. That's why I need your help, Mike. I need you to find her. She'll be able to back me up. She'll be able to tell the cops what happened. She'll be able to tell them I had nothing to do with it. She has short, black spiky hair. And a ring — "

"In her eyebrow. And a spider tattoo on her left upper arm," I said. "I know. You already told me. But how am I going to find her, especially if it's like you say, if she's afraid to come forward?" Or, I thought, if it's like the cops say, if she's your imaginary girlfriend, if you made her up.

"I know you've got doubts, Mike," Vin said. Boy, I could feel my face turn red at that. "But you're the only person I can ask. The cops don't believe me. They're not even going to look for her. They keep pressuring me to tell them who the two guys were — and I don't know. And they keep asking me about a box. When I ask them what box, they say, Come on, Vincent, just tell us where the box is. Do you have it? Do your friends have it? I don't even know what they're talking about. I swear I don't. But they don't believe that, either. I don't even know if my parents believe me. My mother cried when she came down to the police station. My dad — Mike, my dad won't even talk to me. You're the only friend I've got."

I wasn't sure how much of a friend I was. But at least I was here. At least I was listening.

"Do you know anything else about this girl, Vin?"

"Just what I told you. The ring — it's in her right eyebrow, I think." He closed his eyes. "Yeah, I'm pretty sure it's the right. It's silver, not gold. She was kind of pretty. Slim, you know, but not too skinny."

"Have you ever seen her before?"

He shook his head.

"Do you know her name?"

Vin gave me a look. "If I knew her name, I'd tell the cops and then she wouldn't be my imaginary girlfriend anymore."

"But she was in the store?"

"In the back," Vin said. "I saw her. She was in a room that looked like maybe it was a storeroom. The door was open, but not all the way."

I wanted to remind him that Sal hadn't seen her. I wanted to remind him that the man who got shot hadn't mentioned her, either. I wanted to say, But he mentioned *you*, Vin. He identified *you*.

"You think maybe she worked in the store?" I said. But I knew that couldn't be right. The cops would have checked. Or the man who was shot would have said something — unless he hadn't had time to mention her. It said in the paper that he was in critical condition. Maybe he'd just had enough spark in him to identify Vin. But for sure if the girl worked in the store, she would have gone to the police by now. Or someone would have mentioned her.

"All I know," Vin said, "is that I saw her standing there, watching what was going down. She was like a statue. It was like she wasn't even breathing."

She was probably terrified.

"Did she see you?" I said.

"Yeah. She looked right at me. It was her that tipped me to what was going on. I was digging a Coke out of the cooler and I noticed her. Then all of a sudden her eyes went big. She was staring up at the cash. That's when I turned around. That's when I saw the guy with the gun. See, that's the thing, Mike. I didn't even know what was going on until I saw the look in her eyes. That girl saw what happened, Mike. She heard it, same as me. She can tell the cops — she can tell the world — that I had nothing to do with it. That's why you have to find her."

I glanced at the clock on the wall again and pictured Riel starting to pace, out in the reception area.

"Is there anything else that you remember about her, Vin?"

He thought for a moment and then shook his head. I sat there opposite him, watching him, wondering. Finally I asked him the other thing that had been bothering me.

"Vin? Did the cops ask about me?"

"Yeah. They wanted to know if you were there. You know, if you were one of the other two guys."

"What did you tell them?"

He stared at me, his eyes sort of watery, like what I had just asked was going to make him cry.

"What do you think, Mike? You think I'd try to make problems for you? You think I made some kind of deal — Sure, you drop the charges on me or at least reduce them and I'll tell you who did it, it was my friend Mike?" He paused and drew in a deep breath. "You think I don't know how bad I messed up last time? You think I don't know how much that cost me? You think I haven't been sitting here just praying you'd visit or at least arrange a phone call so I could beg you to help me? You think I don't realize how lucky I am that you're even sitting here listening to me? I know I can't change what I did last year, Mike. But I would never jam you up again. Never. No way. I need your help. I'm in trouble and I need your help. That's it."

Part of me wanted to hug him. Can you believe that? After what he'd done to me, I wanted to hug him. I wanted us to be buddies again. I thought about how great it would be if I could undo what had happened, if I could fly backward around the world like Superman and cancel the past six months. Instead, I stood up.

"I gotta go, Vin," I said. "Riel's waiting."

"But you'll find her, right, Mike?"

"I'll do what I can."

"You promise, right?" His voice was higher than usual. Maybe he was telling the truth and maybe he wasn't. But he wasn't faking it about being scared.

"I promise," I said. But as the guard showed me out, I couldn't help wondering: if there had been a girl in the store and if she had seen and heard everything that had happened, why hadn't she gone to the cops? Why hadn't she told them exactly what had happened?

* * *

Riel wasn't pacing. In fact, he didn't even notice when I came back into the reception area. He was standing as far away from the security desk as he could get and he was talking on his cell phone. I couldn't tell who he was talking to, but I heard him say that name again. *Kate.* Why was he talking on the phone all the time to someone named Kate? Finally he flipped his phone shut and dropped it into his jacket pocket. When he saw me standing there, he said, "How's Vin?"

"He's locked up and the cops don't believe him," I said. "How do you think he is?"

Riel have me a sharp look. I knew he didn't like Vin. He couldn't get over what had happened last fall. He handed me an envelope.

"What's this?" I said.

"It's an envelope." No kidding. "Vin left it for you at the desk."

"What's in it?"

"It's addressed to you, Mike, not me." He signed us out on the visitor log. "Come on, let's get out of here."

I opened the envelope on the way back out to the car. There was a single sheet of paper inside. On it was a drawing of a spider. Underneath, Vin had printed, *The tattoo looked like this.* I looked at it and shoved it back into the envelope. Riel glanced at me, but he didn't ask.

CHAPTER FIVE

We made a few stops on the way home. Riel had to pick up some shirts at the dry cleaners and some groceries. His cell phone rang when we were about three blocks from the house. He pulled over and answered it.

"We're just around the corner from the house," he said.

The way he said it made me think it was Susan this time, not the mysterious Kate.

"When?" Riel said. "What did they want?" He listened for longer than it would have taken to drive home. "Did they leave their names?" he said. "Okay. Yeah. I'll let you know." His voice softened a little. "I'll see you tomorrow."

I thought he'd start the car again as soon as he finished the call, but he didn't. Instead he dug something out of his pocket — the card that Detective Canton had given me and that Riel had said he would hang onto, "just in case" — and punched in a phone number. He identified himself to whoever answered and asked, "What do you want to see him about?" I froze when he said that. Detective Canton wanted to see me?

"Is he a suspect?" Riel said.

All of a sudden I was frozen and sweating both at the same time.

"I'm reminding you that he's a juvenile," Riel said. He listened some more. Then he said, "Okay."

He glanced at his watch. "Okay, he'll be there." He closed his phone, dropped it into his pocket and looked at me. "They want to talk to you again."

My mouth was so dry I could hardly ask my question. "Do they think I was involved?"

"They say you're not a suspect. They consider you a person of interest." He said the words like he was spitting out a bad taste in his mouth.

"Person of interest? What does that mean?"

"It means nothing," Riel said. "It's a weasel word. It doesn't have a legal definition. If someone is a suspect, you have to tell him so. Suspects have rights. If you call someone a person of interest, you're not calling him a suspect. You can always say that you just think the person might have information about a police matter. Mostly it intimidates people. But you're just a kid. They have to be careful how they treat you."

"Oh." I wasn't sure I got it. "So they *don't* think I'm a suspect?"

"We're going to straighten that out before we agree to answer any questions," Riel said.

"We?"

He looked at me, his hands on the steering wheel. "I want to be clear on this, Mike," he said. "I don't for one minute think you had anything to do with that convenience store robbery. Vin, that's another matter. I think you have a pretty good idea what I think about him. But the fact that he was with you when he was arrested and the fact that you went to see him — "

"What does that have to do with the police wanting to see me?"

"Canton knows you were with Vin when he was arrested. He knows you've been to see him."

"He does?" But we'd only just come back from there. "How did he find out so fast?"

"The pressure's on, Mike. A pregnant woman was shot."

"She was pregnant?" I didn't remember seeing that in the newspaper.

Riel nodded. "Now she's dead and her husband is in critical condition. Canton and Mancini want to get whoever did it. They've got Vin in custody. They're not buying his story. They're keeping an eye on him. It sounds like they think he knows the other two guys who were involved." His face was grim. "If it was me," he said, "if it was my case, I'd be asking myself if there was a reason other than friendship why you went to see him."

I stared at him.

"I'd wonder if Vin's best friend, who says he was home alone when it happened, might have gone to see Vin to check out what he told the cops."

Geeze.

I looked him straight in the eye. I thought about how his friend on the drug squad had looked him in the eye, too — had looked right at him and had lied to him and how Riel had believed him at first. How was he going to know for sure that I wasn't like his friend?

"I wouldn't lie to you," I said.

"And I wouldn't lie to you, Mike." He turned the key in the ignition. "Let's get this over with, okay?"

* * *

It was just like Riel had said. Canton and Mancini knew I'd been out to see Vin. They said they wanted to talk to me about that.

"Is he a suspect in this case?" Riel said.

"Not at this time," Detective Canton said.

"Is he going to be a suspect in five minutes?" Riel said. He sounded mad.

"We just want to ask Mike a few questions about Vincent Taglia," Detective Canton said.

"It's up to you, Mike, whether or not you want to talk to these detectives," Riel said. "You don't have to if you don't want to."

Detective Canton said, "A woman was killed. Her husband is in grave condition."

Grave? I looked at Riel. As far as I knew, grave was worse than critical.

"Okay," I said. "What do you want to ask me?"

Riel was looking at Detective Canton. He said, "Do it right." So Detective Canton explained my rights. He told me that Riel could stay if I wanted him to. He said I didn't have to answer any questions, but that it would help their investigation if I did. He warned me that anything I said could be used in their investigation. Then he glanced at Riel, who nodded.

"You went to see Vincent," Detective Canton said, finally getting down to it. "Did he tell you anything about what happened that night?"

"He said he didn't do it. He said there was a girl in the store who can prove it."

Detective Mancini, who was standing somewhere behind me, made a noise. It sounded like a snort. Detective Canton kept looking at me.

"Did you even try to find the girl?" I said. "Maybe she works there."

"No one worked there except the man who owned the place and his wife," Detective Canton said. He used the same kind of voice a parent would use on a stubborn kid. "Did Vincent tell you anything about the other two people who were in the store with him when it was robbed?"

"Just that he doesn't know who they were."

"He didn't tell you their names or what they looked like?"

"Just that they were wearing sweatshirts with hoods. He said they were dark blue."

"He didn't tell you why he went into the store with those two guys? He didn't say that maybe they were just fooling around and things got out of hand?"

"What?" He was trying to trip me up. "No! I already told you — *he* already told you. He didn't go into the store *with* them. He went into the store for a Coke and then these two guys came in and they're the ones who robbed the store and shot those people. Vin was scared. That's why he ran. He says he knows it was stupid, but that's what he did."

"You told us that you and Vincent hadn't seen

each other in months," Detective Canton said.

"That's right."

"But the day after Vincent was seen running out of a store where two people were shot, you were found with him."

Found with him? What did that mean?

"I wasn't found with him. He came up to me in the park after work. He told me what happened. He said he was afraid you wouldn't believe him. We were going to my place to talk to John. He used to be a cop — police officer. I figured he would know what to do."

Detective Canton just sat there for a few moments, staring at me.

"This isn't the first time Vincent has been in trouble, is it, Mike?" he said finally.

I just shrugged.

Detective Canton stared at me a little longer.

"What else did you and Vincent talk about, Mike?"

"Nothing."

"What was in the envelope?"

"What?" They knew about that, too?

"That was personal correspondence," Riel said.

"He wrote you a letter?" Detective Canton said.

"You don't have to answer that if you don't want to, Mike," Riel said.

"He drew me a picture," I said.

"A picture?" Detective Canton said.

"Of a tattoo." I pulled it out of my pocket and showed it to him. "He said the girl had that tattoo."

"The girl?" Detective Canton said. "Or maybe one of his buddies, one of the guys who was with him in the store? Does he want you to deliver a message, Mike? Is that why he drew you that picture?"

"What? No!"

Detective Canton did his cop stare again.

"Were you in that convenience store with Vincent Taglia two nights ago?" he said.

Riel stood up. "That's it," he said. "Come on, Mike. We're going home." When I didn't move fast enough, he grabbed my arm. "Come on."

Detective Canton kept staring at me as we left.

Riel didn't say a word until we were in the car. He cranked the key in the ignition like he was trying to twist Canton's arm off. Then he turned to me and said, "You didn't phone anybody that night, nobody phoned you or even phoned to talk to me and ended up talking to you, nothing like that?"

"No," I said. Was he starting to doubt me? "I watched TV. I taped a show for Susan."

"You did?" Riel said. She must not have mentioned it to him. "Where's the tape now?"

"Susan has it." I'd been wondering about that tape, about whether I should say something about it. "Do you think it would help me, you know, if they really think I had something to do with that robbery?"

"Maybe," Riel said. "Although they could always say that you programmed the VCR to tape it while you were out."

"But I didn't," I said. "I watched the show while I was taping it."

"We'll get the tape from Susan," Riel said. "Just in case. And Mike? If you want my advice, I think you should stay away from Vin. If you don't, they're going to make things hard for you."

They were already making things hard for me.

* * *

As soon as we got home, I looked for the videotape that I had made for Susan, but I couldn't find it.

"She must have taken it home," Riel said. "She'll probably call me tonight if she gets a break. I'll ask her then. If not, I'll talk to her tomorrow. Don't worry."

But I did worry. I worried so much that I couldn't sleep that night. I kept thinking about Vin and about the cops trying to scare me. And about Vin again. He would never have told them that I was involved. But they didn't believe him about anything — they didn't believe he hadn't been involved, they didn't believe that he didn't know the two guys who had come into the store after him, and they didn't believe that there was a girl in the store. So why would they believe him if he said his (former) best friend hadn't been there? Riel was on my side, though, I was sure of it. That made me feel safe. I knew (well, I was pretty sure) that he'd stick up for me.

Then I thought about Rebecca, who was mad at me and who I should have called when I got home to see exactly how mad — although the fact that she hadn't phoned me told me something.

And I thought about Sal, who was also mad at me

and who had things going on in his life that all of a sudden I knew nothing about. My head was crammed full of everyone I knew and what they thought of me. I couldn't sleep and couldn't sleep, and the next thing I knew, Riel was pounding on my door telling me that if I didn't get out of bed right now, I was going to be late for school.

* * *

I wasn't late — not even close — because, of course, there was no way Riel would let me be late. I got to school at pretty much the regular time, which was a full ten minutes before the bell rang. Rebecca was standing in front of the school. She zeroed in on me as I came down the sidewalk. Her face was so serious that I started to get a sick feeling. All I could think was, She's still mad at me, she's going to dump me.

She walked over to me, still with a serious face, which was so pale that every single freckle on her nose and cheeks stood right out. Rebecca told me one time that when she has to do something hard — like stand up in front of the class and make a speech, or like break up with someone — she can't sleep the night before. She looked like she hadn't slept at all last night.

"I'm sorry, Mike," she said.

My stomach did a back flip. Jen had started her dump-Mike speech the same way: *I'm sorry, Mike . . .*

"I shouldn't have walked out yesterday the way I did," she said.

No, you should have dumped me right then and there, in the middle of the cafeteria, with practically the whole school watching. If you're going to do something like that, you might as well go big. Make a statement: Hey, world, Mike and I are through.

Then she said, "Forgive me?"

What?

I stared at her.

"Forgive you for what?"

"For walking out on you," she said, giving me a look, probably wondering if I had even noticed that she'd been mad at me in the first place. She'd told me a couple of times that guys were emotion-blind (and maybe five or six other kinds of blind). Like when guys can't see that a woman is upset, or when they don't read the vibes the way women do. She looked like she was thinking that now — I was acting like a guy; in other words, I didn't have a clue what was going on. And me? I was running her words through my head before I said anything, because I was sure I must have heard wrong. *She* wanted *me* to forgive *her?*

"It's okay," I said finally. She relaxed a little, which is how I knew I had said the right thing. "You were mad at me."

"Yeah," she said. "I was. But that's no excuse. I shouldn't have lost my temper and I shouldn't have walked out on you. You can't solve problems that way." She caught my hand and squeezed it. "I tried to call you yesterday after school, but you weren't around."

"You should have left a message," I said, even though I knew why she hadn't. Rebecca always got a little nervous when she phoned Riel's house. She said it made her squirm when Riel answered instead of me. He was her history teacher and for some reason that always made her freeze up around him. So when she called and no one answered, she almost never left a message. She said it made her feel funny to think that Mr. Riel (she always referred to him like that) might listen to something she said to me. A few times, but only if it was urgent, she'd say, "Could Mike please call Rebecca?" really fast into the phone and then hang up. After every time she called me, she said, "You have to get a cell phone, Mike." I was saving up for one.

"I called a couple of times, then I had to go to band practice," she said now, "so you wouldn't have been able to call me back anyway." Mr. Korchak, our music teacher at school, had a rule about cell phones during band practice: Turn them OFF, ladies and gentlemen. "Practice went late, so by the time I could call you again . . . " She shrugged, but I knew what she meant. I didn't have a phone in my room. Riel would have picked up. "Anyway, I wanted to talk to you face-to-face. We're okay, right? We're not breaking up or anything?"

"Geeze, no."

She smiled at me. I love it when Rebecca smiles. It makes me feel warm, like I'm standing in the sun.

"So, do you really think that Vin had nothing to do with that shooting?"

"I went to see him yesterday." I said it slowly, afraid that she would have a problem with that. But she just nodded. "He says he wasn't involved. He swears it." She waited. Maybe she's right about women picking up on vibes better than guys, because she seemed to know there was more. "I *want* to believe him, Rebecca. I can't help it. I've known him since forever," I said. "But *do* I believe him?" It was the question that just wouldn't leave me alone. "I don't know. That's why I have to find the girl."

"What girl?"

I told her what Vin had told me.

"And this girl hasn't gone to the police?"

"Vin says the police don't even believe she exists."

"And you do?"

I shrugged. "The thing is, Rebecca, I keep seeing it this way. Suppose it was me who'd run out of that store. And suppose, crazy as it might sound to some people, I really wasn't involved."

"That doesn't sound crazy to me."

I wanted to kiss her right then. "Suppose I ran because I was scared, just like Vin says he was. And suppose I really found that money the way Vin says he did — "

"What money?"

I told her about the cash the cops had found on Vin. She didn't say anything.

"Suppose it was me instead of Vin," I said. "Suppose, sure, I'd been stupid, but that I hadn't done anything wrong. But suppose it looked really bad for me. And suppose no one believed me. I'd need a friend, right? Someone who could help me."

"I'd help you," she said.

I didn't doubt it for a minute. I stared into her brown eyes.

"For Vin, I'm the one," I said. "Maybe things have been lousy between Vin and me lately, but he's my friend." It kept coming back to that. I kept thinking it and saying it, so it had to be true. "And I'm the only person who's willing to help him."

"By finding this girl?"

I nodded.

"Did you tell Mr. Riel?"

"About the girl? Yeah. He doesn't believe it, either."

"Did you tell him you were going to help Vin?"

I shook my head. I didn't tell her the rest of it, about the cops pressuring me, and Riel telling me to keep clear of Vin.

The warning bell rang. Rebecca looked up at the school doors.

"I have band practice at lunchtime," she said. She played the saxophone and she'd stuck to it long enough that she'd aced the tryouts. I played sax, too, but not very well, for sure not well enough to make band. I was beginning to think that music wasn't my thing. I hadn't figured out yet what was. "Meet me after school," she said. "We'll figure something out."

"We will?" I was definitely having hearing problems today. "You mean, as in you and me?"

"As in you and *I*," she said, smiling. She went up on tiptoes to kiss me on the cheek, right there in front of the school.

CHAPTER SIX

"I had an idea," Rebecca said when she met me at my locker after school. "We were playing volleyball in gym when it hit me."

"Maybe you should have ducked," I said. I crammed some books into my locker, took some other books out and jammed them into my backpack.

"I'm serious," Rebecca said as we headed for the stairs so that she could go to her locker, but she didn't tell me right away what her idea was because by then we were on the second-floor landing and Sal was standing there. He turned away as soon as he saw me and hurried past us.

"Hi, Sal," Rebecca said, her voice sweet and friendly, like always.

Sal turned back. "Hi, Rebecca," he said, focusing hard on her so he wouldn't have to look at me. Then he spun around and practically ran all the way down the stairs.

"You want to go after him and try to talk to him?" Rebecca said, watching him.

I shook my head. "He's probably on his way to work. I'll catch up with him later, when he has more time." Rebecca didn't say anything, but I bet she saw right through me. She always gave me that feeling. "So, what was your idea?" I said.

* * *

The way Rebecca figured it, if the girl Vin said he saw in the store had been where Vin said she was, in the storeroom, and if she didn't work at the store

— and we knew she didn't because the cops had said the man and his wife ran the place alone — then that was, as she put it, "significant."

"Let's agree that ordinary customers don't usually go into a store's back room," she said.

"Okay," I said.

"So that means that if we're going to assume that the girl was really there — "

If we're going to assume.

" — then she wasn't an ordinary customer. She must have known the people who ran the store. And if she knew the people well enough that they let her go in the storeroom, then maybe we can also assume that she's been in the store more than once. Makes sense, right?"

"Okay," I said. I wondered where she was going with this.

"So, let's assume that she *has* been in the store before. And then let's assume that if that's true, maybe someone else saw her in the store at some point. Maybe they remember her. From the way Vin described her, she sounds like the kind of person you'd remember."

"So what we have to do — "

"Is make like cops. Ask around. See what we can find out." She smiled at me. "Come on. Are we going or what?"

There was that word again. *We.*

* * *

You'd think it would be easy enough — you walk up to a person, or several people, you describe a girl, and you ask that person or those people if they've ever seen her.

Well, if that's what you think, you should try it. Go up to the guy who's behind the cash at the gas station that's kitty-corner to the convenience store where the woman and the man got shot and say, "Excuse me, but I'm looking for a girl." Describe the girl and ask him, "Have you seen her?" Check out the way the guy, who at first looked bored, now starts to look suspicious. Check out the way his eyes narrow. Check out the way he says, "What if I have?"

Rebecca and I went to the gas station first because it was the only place around that wasn't either a house or a low-rise apartment building. The convenience store was a couple of blocks north of Danforth on the corner of a street in the middle of a residential neighbourhood. It was the place where all the people in all the houses and apartment buildings around it would go if they'd suddenly run out of milk or cigarettes or if their kids wanted a candy bar or a bag of chips. There was a gas station on the corner diagonally opposite, and that was the sum total of the businesses in the immediate area.

The other reason Rebecca and I went to the gas station first was that we figured there was always someone there — either the guy who was standing behind the cash now or whoever replaced him when he went home. We thought the guy behind the cash might be the kind of person who took an interest in what went on around him. At least, we thought that before we went into the gas station.

As soon as we got inside, I knew we were wrong. This wasn't one of those gas stations that have stores in them, you know, the way some of them sell snacks and juice and pop and cigarettes. Some of them even have a Tim's inside that sells coffee and doughnuts and soup and sandwiches. Instead it was a cramped, square room attached to a garage where, I guess, there was a mechanic who did repairs. In the tiny room was a counter behind which was jammed a bored-looking guy and two TV monitors. One monitor showed the gas pumps, so the guy could see what was going on out there. The other was tuned to a talk show, but with the sound turned way down. The guy behind the counter wasn't looking at either monitor. He was reading a newspaper, the one that always ran pictures of girls in bikinis. Even though a bell rang over the door when we opened it, he didn't look up. He kept right on reading. Yeah, this was a guy who took a real interest in what went on around him.

Once we were inside, I didn't see any point in talking to him. But Rebecca said, "Excuse me," and the guy looked up. Rebecca gave me a look that said, *Well, go on.* So I described to him the girl that Vin had described to me and asked if he had seen her.

I was rewarded by the guy's totally bored look. And his genius question: "What if I have?"

"Well, we're looking for her," Rebecca said.

The guy seemed to like that Rebecca had answered. It gave him an excuse to focus on her and ignore me. In fact, he seemed to enjoy looking at her, and I couldn't blame him. She's really pretty. But I didn't like the way he was staring at her.

"Why?" he said.

"Why are we looking for her?" Rebecca smiled at the guy, probably to soften him up. "She's a friend of a friend. We heard she lives around here. We thought maybe she could help us with something."

It sounded pretty lame, but the guy behind the counter didn't seem to mind. If you ask me, he was thinking up things Rebecca could help *him* with.

"So, have you seen her?" Rebecca said.

"No," the guy said.

"You're sure?" Rebecca said. She described the girl again.

The guy shook his head. "Hey, gorgeous," he said to Rebecca, "what's your name?"

"Thank you for your time," Rebecca said. She grabbed my hand and pulled me out of the place. "What a creep," she muttered when we were outside again.

"Yeah. And he was probably our best shot. I mean, he just sits there all day, every day."

Rebecca looked around. There were houses up and down the street in two different directions: north–south and east–west. Kids were playing outside in front of some of them. There were a few grown-ups outside, too, most of them women, most of them with their eyes zeroed in on little kids. An old man came down the street with a dog on a leash. It was one of those small dogs that looks like a barrel on legs and has a pushed-in face. The man turned up the front walk of a house a couple of doors away from the convenience store. He tied the dog's leash to the porch railing and then sat on the porch steps, easing himself down, like it hurt every inch of the way.

"Come on," Rebecca said. She started for the old guy's house.

"Hey," I said. I had to run to catch her because she had broken away from me so suddenly and was moving so fast. "Where are you going?"

"People with dogs are out at least twice a day walking them," she said. "Old guys with dogs, they've got nothing better to do. They're always out, especially in nice weather like this. They see everything."

Right.

When we'd first got there, Rebecca had been cranked about the gas station. Gas stations are open long hours, she'd said. People who work in gas stations see all kinds of things that regular people don't see.

Uh-huh.

She crossed the street and sauntered up the old man's walk.

"Hello," she said.

The old man looked at her. He didn't get up, but he did smile. Guys always smile at Rebecca. It doesn't matter how old they are.

"You selling something?" he said. "Because if you are, I have to warn you, I'm not a soft touch. Well, unless you're selling Girl Guide cookies. I sure do like those. The vanilla ones in particular. I keep telling them, sell boxes of just vanilla instead of those mixed boxes of chocolate and vanilla, and I'd buy a gross."

"If they're gross, why would he buy them?" I whispered to Rebecca.

"A gross is twelve dozen," she said quietly.

Who knew?

"But I don't suppose you're a Girl Guide," the old man said. "And I don't suppose you're selling Girl Guide cookies, are you?" He glanced at me when he said that. His expression wasn't nearly as friendly when he looked me over as it had been when he'd checked out Rebecca.

"We're not selling anything," Rebecca said. "We're looking for someone."

The old guy peered a little harder at Rebecca now. "There's a lot of people looking for someone around here," he said. "There was a woman shot and killed here just last week, and her husband is in the hospital. He was shot, too. I heard he's in rough shape."

"That's terrible," Rebecca said. When I started to say something — "We know." — she squeezed my hand. I got the message.

"The police were around," the old man said. "They said it was three young fellows who did it. They said they know who one of them is and that they're looking for the other two." He looked sharply at me.

"We're not looking for a guy," Rebecca said. "We're looking for a girl." The man shifted his eyes back to her. "We found this wallet in the little park down the street," she said. She pulled a brown-and-tan leather wallet from her purse. I knew for a fact that it was hers. "There was a little kid in the park. He was pretty sure he saw the girl who might have dropped it. But there's no name in it and no ID. Just twenty-five dollars. Since she dropped it in the park right near here, we thought maybe she lived around here."

She looked so sincere. That's probably because she's an honest person — well, apart from the occasional little white lie, like the one she was telling right now. It also doesn't hurt that she's so pretty. It was making it easy for the old man to want to believe her. In fact, he looked impressed. He was probably one of those people who think that kids are nothing but trouble, so he was probably surprised that here were a couple of kids who were trying to do the right thing.

"What does this girl look like?" he said.

Rebecca was hitting it off so well with the old guy that I decided to let her do all the talking. She gave him the description that Vin had given me.

"Spiky black hair?" the old man echoed. "The black I get. But the spiky part — didn't that go out a few years ago?"

"Mostly," Rebecca agreed. "But some people just go with whatever they like or whatever they think makes the statement they're trying to make."

"Tell me," the old guy said, "when a nice-looking girl puts a ring through her eyebrow, what kind of statement is she trying to make?"

"I'm not a hundred percent sure," Rebecca said after thinking for a moment. "Maybe she's saying, I can handle the pain. You know, maybe she's saying she's tough."

The old guy nodded. "You could be right," he said. "Anyway, it fits."

It fits? What did that mean?

Rebecca must have been wondering the same thing, because she turned her head and gave me a warning look, like I should keep my mouth shut and let her go with the flow.

"So you've seen her around?" she said to the old man. "You've seen the girl that the boy in the park described to us?"

"I've seen her," the old man said. "But if you ask me, it would be justice if you kept that wallet."

Rebecca waited. I was dying to ask the old man what he meant, but Rebecca was patient.

"She was in the store," he said, "the one I was telling you about, where the woman and her husband got shot. Cecilia Lee, that was the woman's name. A really nice woman. A lot younger than her husband. I heard they met through one of those international dating services. She came here from China especially to marry him."

That surprised me. The newspaper hadn't included any of those details, just the main facts.

"She was a hard worker, too," the old man said. "They both were. They kept that store open seven days a week, six in the morning until midnight. It's tough for little places like that to keep afloat. They're up against the big guys that are open twenty-four hours a day. It was different when the big grocery stores used to close at six or nine at night and didn't even open on Sunday. And then there's places like 7–Eleven." He shook his head. "Fifteen or twenty years ago, there were corner stores every couple of blocks around here and people went regularly to the one closest to their house. But not anymore. Now they're closing one by one. Lots of the neighbourhood places just fold, and then people buy them and convert them into regular houses."

Rebecca nodded. She had a serious expression on her face, like she was listening closely to every word.

"The girl you described," he said. "She was in the store, oh, three, maybe four months ago. I was in there buying milk for my coffee and right away, as soon as I went through the door, I saw her. You couldn't miss her with that spiky hair and that hardware through her eyebrow. And you know what she was doing in there?"

Rebecca shook her head.

"Treating herself to a five-finger discount."

It took me a couple of seconds to get what he meant. She'd been shoplifting.

"What's the matter with kids, anyway?" the old

man said. "They see something, they just take it, like it was free, like someone didn't have to pay for it in the first place. Well, I grabbed her good, let me tell you. To a young lady like you, I may look like I'm over the hill, but I still have a few good muscles and some pretty good reflexes. I grabbed her and I told Mrs. Lee she'd better call the police." He shook his head again. "But she didn't."

"She let the girl go?" Rebecca said.

"For all I know," the old man said. "I told her to call the police, but she just shook her head and said she would take care of it."

"What did she do?"

The old man shrugged. "Nothing, I guess. I argued with her about it — it really got to me how the girl just smirked when Mrs. Lee said she didn't want to call the police. Then I left the store." He thought a moment. "The girl didn't take off right away, like you'd expect. I don't know what happened after that. I watched a while from my window, you know, to make sure everything was okay, but I never saw the girl come out of the store. Maybe she left when I turned away for a minute, I don't know. Tell you what, though. Her husband was angry when he found out."

"He was there, too?" Rebecca said.

The old man shook his head. "I mentioned it to him the next time I was in the store. He got pretty angry. He would have called the police for sure. Yes sir, he would have taught that girl a lesson."

"So," Rebecca said slowly, "I guess you don't

know if she lives around here?"

"Maybe she does," the old man said. "But I doubt it. Ticker and I are out and about every day." Ticker must have been the little barrel with legs that was leashed to the porch railing. "I bet we know pretty much everyone in the area. But I only ever saw the girl that one time."

Rebecca thanked the old man for his time and flashed him a big, sincere thank-you smile. The old man didn't even look at me, which was good. It saved me having to pretend something I didn't feel.

"So, that was good," Rebecca said as we walked away.

"Right," I said. "That was really productive." I was being sarcastic.

Rebecca looped an arm through mine. "You should be happy," she said.

"But we didn't find out the girl's name and we didn't find out where she lives."

Rebecca stopped and turned so that she could look me in the eye.

"Don't you get it, Mike? The girl really exists," she said. "That man saw her. He saw a girl in the store who looks exactly like Vin described. Vin was telling you the truth."

"I get it," I said. "But what good does it do when the cops don't believe it?"

"We could go to the police. We could get them to talk to the old man."

I shuddered at the thought of going anywhere near Detectives Canton and Mancini. Besides, what good would it do? "He'd just tell them what he told us," I said. "That he saw the girl around a couple of months ago, but that he hasn't seen her since. In fact, he's pretty sure she hasn't been around since then because he's out and around all the time and he would have noticed — and, oh, by the way, that one time he saw her, she was boosting stuff from the store." I shook my head. "Like that's going to turn the cops into real believers! If anything, they're going to think maybe the girl was in on it or that maybe she's Vin's real girlfriend instead of his imaginary girlfriend and if she'd steal, she'd also lie, so they wouldn't believe her even if they decided to look for her." I felt so bitter that it took a few seconds for me to register the hurt look on Rebecca's face. I pulled her close to me. "I'm sorry," I said. "You did great. You're amazing. It's just that I thought finding out about the girl would make things better. Instead, it looks like it's not going to make any difference at all."

Rebecca slipped an arm around my waist and we walked that way to the subway, holding each other.

CHAPTER SEVEN

I heard Riel's voice as soon as I opened the front door. It sounded like he was talking to someone in the kitchen. At first I didn't know who it was. I couldn't even tell whether he was talking on the phone or if there was someone in there with him. I heard him say, "Why does this have to be so complicated? Can't a guy just say he changed his mind without everyone wanting to analyze it to death?" Then he said, "I know I told her I was through. Are you going to tell me that she never said anything like that? Or you? You never in your life said you were through?"

I stopped where I was, in the front hall, with the front door still open. What was he talking about? Through with who? Susan? Boy, I sure hoped not.

"You're asking the wrong person, John," a familiar voice said. It was Dave Jones, a cop friend of Riel's. "For me it's the other way around. You know how many times I came this close to getting married to some perfectly nice woman and then she said she was through? You know how many times I wish she hadn't said that?"

"Probably almost as many times as you've said you're glad she did," Riel said.

Dave Jones laughed, but when he spoke again, his voice was serious. "You should tell Susan. You should do it now."

Tell Susan what? What was going on?

"I talked to Kate again," Riel said. "I'm going to go and see her. Depending on what she says, I'll talk to Susan. But there's no reason to upset her until I know for sure where I stand."

I'd heard him say that before — to Kate. I started to get a bad feeling about Riel and Susan. I backed up so that I could close the front door — you know, slam it so that he would think I'd just come through the door and I hadn't heard what he was saying. Instead, I bumped into the new little table that Susan had bought for the front hall. It sat in what used to be empty space — and because I was used to that empty space, I kept knocking into the stupid table. It didn't make a lot of noise, but it was enough to make Riel call out, "Mike, is that you?" You could tell he used to be a police detective, because he knew there was no way that Susan would ever bang into that table the way I did.

"Yeah," I said. "I'm home," trying to make it sound like I'd just got there.

"Do me a favour," Riel called. "Take the garbage out front, will you? The cans and the bottles, too, Mike. They're being picked up tomorrow." Which, of course, I knew, but which Riel was probably going to remind me about every week because once, just once, I had forgotten the cans and the bottles, which get picked up every two weeks for recycling, and because of that, Riel didn't trust me to ever remember.

I went out of my way to make noise closing the door behind me so that they'd know I was gone.

That was the whole point — give Mike something to do to get him out of the house so that Riel could finish his (private) conversation with Dave Jones.

They came out the front door while I was hauling the garbage and the blue boxes from the back of the house to the curb. Riel walked Dave to his car and they stood there for a moment talking before Dave finally got into his car and drove away. Riel stood on the sidewalk and watched him go. Then he turned to me and said, "Where have you been?"

"Out with Rebecca. Is everything okay?"

Riel looked at me. "Why wouldn't it be?" he said.

"No reason."

"You're going to have to get your own supper tonight. I have to go somewhere." He didn't say where. He didn't have to. He'd already told Dave Jones that he was going to go and see Kate.

I was halfway through saying it was no problem when he jogged up the front walk and into the house. He came out a few seconds later, his car keys dangling from one hand. He left. Two hours later Susan let herself into the house. She stood in the front hall and called his name. Something about her seemed different. It took me a moment to realize what it was. She was angry.

"He's not here," I told her.

"Do you know where he is?" she said. She sounded different, too, like she was doing her best not to take out whatever she was angry about on me.

I told her I didn't. I also told her that I didn't know when he'd be back.

"Did you try his cell?" I said.

"I can't get through to him," she said. "I keep getting his voicemail, and he hasn't returned my calls." That seemed to make her even angrier. "I think he must have turned his phone off."

She went into the living room and sat down on the couch. For a few moments, she just sat there. Then she picked up a magazine and started to flick through the pages without even looking at them.

I thought about calling Riel's cell and leaving a message to warn him. But he would have to listen to all of Susan's messages before he got to mine, and by then he'd already know she was mad. Instead, I asked Susan if she wanted me to make her a cup of tea. Susan was a big tea drinker.

"That would be nice, Mike," she said. "Thanks."

I made the tea and brought it to her. She was flicking through the magazine pages more slowly now, so I figured she wasn't as mad anymore.

"Did John ask you about that tape?" I said.

"Tape?" She looked confused for a moment, probably because she was still thinking about where Riel was. "Oh," she said. "The video. Yes, he did. And I realized that I forgot to thank you for making it, Mike. It was especially nice how you skipped the commercials. I hate watching commercials."

"Yeah, well it would have been easier," I said, "if *someone*" — meaning Riel — "had a VCR that was younger than me instead of older than me. The ones they have now, you can program them to skip commercials. But not this one." I nodded to the

VCR that sat next to Riel's TV. It was a real dinosaur. "The only way you can skip the commercials is if you sit there and stop the VCR when the commercials start, and then start the tape again when the commercials are over."

"I could have just fast-forwarded, Mike," Susan said.

"I know." But I also knew that commercials bugged her. And it was the grand finale of her favourite show, plus a behind-the-scenes special on the show. She hadn't asked me to tape it for her — I knew she was going to miss it because she and Riel had something else planned. And it wasn't like I was doing anything else that night. "It was no big deal to do it without commercials," I said. "So, John asked you about it, right? You still have it?"

"I lent it to a friend of mine," she said. "But don't worry. I called her and left a message. I'll get it back — not that I think you'll need it, Mike. I think John is right. I think the police are just trying to scare you. But I'll get it back for sure. I promise."

I hoped she was right.

* * *

When the phone rang later that night, I scrambled to answer it. It was Rebecca. She said she was glad I had picked up. I told her I was glad she'd called.

"'Cause you adore me, huh?" she said.

"That, and because John and Susan just had a fight," I said.

There was a little pause at the end of the line. Then Rebecca said, "But they're getting married."

"That's what they were fighting about. The wedding, I mean, not whether or not they're getting married." At least, they weren't fighting about that yet.

"What part of the wedding?" Rebecca said, more interested than I would have been if I wasn't living with Riel.

"It started out being the menu."

"For the reception, you mean," Rebecca said.

"They were supposed to go somewhere together and taste different stuff, but Riel didn't show up."

"And Susan got mad, huh?"

"Not right away."

Susan had calmed down a lot by the time Riel walked through the door. When she asked him how come he didn't show up, you couldn't tell that she had been mad before. I think she was ready to give him the benefit of the doubt. But her face tensed up fast when he said that something had come up, he'd had to go downtown, and he'd forgotten all about the caterer. I felt kind of sick. He was lying to her. It hadn't come up — he had arranged it — and it hadn't been last-minute. I called your cell, Susan said, but you didn't answer. Oh yeah, he said, he'd left his cell phone in the car. In the *car?* she said. You never leave your cell phone in the car. Yeah, well he'd done it today and he was sorry, really, it was just he had all these things on his mind. Right, she said. She still wasn't mad. That came later, when she pulled out a pile of menus and the binder that she carried around all the time to keep track of everything for the wedding.

Susan's binder was thicker than my English and history binders combined. She opened it and took out a sheet of paper that was covered with her handwriting, which looked pretty neat to me, considering that she was a doctor, and said, "Okay, here's what you missed . . . "

She started to go through all the different things she had tasted and what she thought about them and what she thought the guests would think about them and how they might stand up (as she put it) if it turned out to be really hot the day they got married. It sounded boring to me. To Riel, too, I guess — or maybe he was thinking about Kate (but I didn't say that to Rebecca because I didn't want her to think something bad about Riel that maybe wasn't even true) — because suddenly there was Susan's voice, sharp, saying, "John, are you even listening to me?"

And then there was Riel who, really, I figured should have been smarter, saying, "Why don't you just go with what you like?"

The next thing you know, they were acting like they were already married. I'd never heard her yell at him before, but she yelled then, mostly about how he was leaving everything to her and she didn't think that was a good way to start what was supposed to be a life partnership, blah-blah-blah. Riel tried to apologize, but she wouldn't listen. She ended up banging out the front door. Next thing you know, her car was pulling away from the curb.

Riel hung around the house for about an hour, calling her — at least I assumed it was Susan he was calling — but not getting any answer. Then he left the house, too.

"You think she's going to call off the wedding?" I said to Rebecca.

"I think Mr. Riel better pay more attention to her," Rebecca said.

"Yeah." I hoped he would. I liked Susan. I liked how she made him happy. "So what's up?"

"The funeral is tomorrow."

"What funeral?"

"The one for Cecilia Lee, the woman who was shot. I read in the paper that the funeral is tomorrow morning. We should go."

"What for?"

I heard a little sigh on the other end of the line.

"We want to find that girl, right, Mike?"

"Yeah, but — "

"Maybe she'll turn up at the funeral."

Boy, where had she got that idea? "That old guy caught her stealing from the store, Rebecca. Why would she go to the funeral of someone she was trying to steal from?"

"He also said that Mrs. Lee didn't call the police. Instead, she let her go," Rebecca said. "And we're assuming Vin is telling you the truth about that day, even if he isn't, right?" She waited for me to say something, so I said, yeah, right. "Well, if Vin *is* telling the truth, then that girl was in the storeroom at the back of the store when it happened.

That means that she knows that the woman who caught her stealing, but *didn't* call the cops on her, got shot — maybe she feels bad about that. So bad she'll show up at the funeral."

"If she felt bad about it, she'd have gone to the police and told them what she saw."

I heard another sigh, except that this one sounded impatient. For some reason, it reminded me of Susan.

"You got any better ideas, Mike?"

Well . . . "No."

"The funeral is at eleven. I have a spare and then lunch."

"I have math and then lunch."

"You think you can get Mr. Riel to let you skip one class?"

I doubted it, but I said, "I'll meet you behind school right after second period, okay?"

"Okay," she said. "And, Mike? It's a funeral. You're going to have to dress nice."

"No problem."

* * *

I had been hoping to sneak out of the house the next morning without being noticed, but when does that ever happen?

Susan spotted me first. She was walking through the living room, a cup of coffee in one hand and the newspaper in the other. She smiled at me. She looked a lot happier than she had when she'd left the house last night. I had heard the front door open a little before eleven. Then I'd heard footsteps and Riel knocked on my bedroom door and poked his head in. He'd looked more relaxed. But all he'd said was, "Goodnight, Mike." He hadn't told me that Susan was with him. It was obvious from how she looked now that she had forgiven him.

"Mike," she said. "You're all dressed up."

That brought Riel out of the kitchen to take a look. He was in his usual teacher clothes — casual slacks and a sports shirt. He gave me a once-over and said, "What's up, Mike? You got a court date I don't know about?"

I thought about making something up, but that never worked with Riel. Nine times out of ten, he could tell I was lying. The other ten percent of the time, he eventually found out and then he was disappointed in me for not being straight in the first place. So these days I pretty much told him the truth.

"Rebecca and I want to go to that woman's funeral," I said. "Rebecca has a spare, so it's okay for her. But I don't. Can you write me a note?"

"Funeral?" he said. "What woman?"

"The woman who was shot at the convenience store."

Riel and Susan exchanged glances.

"Why do you want to go to her funeral?" Riel said. "You didn't even know her. Not that that's a reason not to go. I wouldn't be surprised if a lot of people from the area showed up, given how she died."

"I just thought, you know, since Vin was in the store and since Sal was the one who called the police . . . " I shrugged and hoped he'd leave it at that.

I didn't want to tell him the real reason I was going.

Riel surprised me. He didn't say no right away. He said, "What class would you miss?"

"Math. Then I have lunch. We'll be back at school for the first period after lunch. I promise."

Riel disappeared into the kitchen. When he came back out again, he handed me a note.

"Check in with Mr. Tran before the end of the day," he said. "Find out what you missed and make sure you get your math homework from him. And check in with me when you get back. I have a prep period after lunch today."

I said I would.

* * *

Rebecca was waiting outside for me at the end of second period. She had on a black skirt and a grey blouse and, even dressed for a funeral, she looked terrific.

"I don't think this is going to do any good," I said.

"We'll see," she said. I didn't argue with her.

The service was held in a church. The minister said that Mrs. Lee had been attending regularly since she'd come to this country. I heard someone behind me whisper that it was a shame her husband never came with her. Something in the way she said it made me think that she didn't think highly of Mr. Lee. Someone else said that the minister had gone to the hospital a couple of times hoping to talk to Mr. Lee about what he wanted in the funeral service, but that Mr. Lee was in such serious condition that he finally had to go ahead without consulting him.

The church was packed, which made it hard to get a good look at everyone who was there. There were a lot of Chinese people, but a lot of other people, too. As soon as the service ended and they took the casket outside to load it into the hearse for the drive to the cemetery, Rebecca grabbed me by the hand and pulled me down the aisle. We stood outside and watched people as they came out of the church.

"I don't see any short black spiky hair," I said, although I saw a lot of black suits and black shirts, black sweaters and black blouses, black shoes and black hats. "And if her tattoo is where Vin says it is, it's going to be covered up." It was a cool day, for May. Everyone was wearing long sleeves. Most people had on jackets or sweaters. Besides, even I wouldn't go to a funeral with a tattoo of a spider on display, assuming I had a tattoo of a spider.

Rebecca kept scanning people as they went by us, but I could see that she was getting discouraged. Suddenly she grabbed my arm and said, "What else did Vin say about the girl?"

"What?"

"Short black spiky hair, a tattoo of a spider, pierced eyebrow. What else?"

"Geeze, Rebecca, let go."

"Mike, what else?"

I tried to think. "Nothing. Other than she's slim and she's pretty."

"Pretty." She shook her head impatiently. "He thought Cat was pretty." Cat, the girl Vin had been going with for a while, was about as pretty as a poisonous snake. "Look at that girl, Mike. You think *she's* pretty?"

"What?"

She pointed to a thin girl with short blond hair. She was dressed kind of like Rebecca, in a black skirt, except that she also had on a black top — a blouse — and she had a big bag over her shoulder, the kind girls cram with all kinds of stuff they think they might need because you never know, right? She was definitely pretty, but there was no way I was going to tell Rebecca that. A guy never tells his girlfriend that he thinks another girl is pretty, not if he wants to keep her as a girlfriend.

"Come on, Mike, do you think she's pretty?"

"Not nearly as pretty as you," I said.

"Would Vin think she's pretty?"

"What?"

But Rebecca was moving away from me now, toward the girl. She said something, but I couldn't hear what it was. The girl turned away from her and started to move through the crowd. Rebecca went after her.

"Rebecca!" I called. "Wait up."

Rebecca looked over her shoulder at me, then she took off after the girl, who by then had been swallowed up by the crowd. I had to run to catch up. I found Rebecca around the side of the church. She was standing alone, looking all around as if she had lost something and was trying to figure out where it could be.

"What's going on?" I said.

"I think that was her."

"You think who was who?"

"That girl I spoke to. It could have been her."

"But that girl had blond hair and it wasn't spiky."

"Hair doesn't *come* spiky, Mike," Rebecca said patiently. "It's not like wavy hair or curly hair. You put stuff in it to make it stick up. Besides, it's a funeral. You don't want to look weird at a funeral."

"Yeah, but the colour — "

"You never heard of hair dye? And you know what else, Mike? She had marks on her eyebrow, right here." She pointed to her own right eyebrow. "It was a piercing. She took the ring out and she put makeup over the spot, but you could tell it was a piercing." Well, maybe Rebecca could tell.

"What did you say to her?"

"I asked her if she was here because she knew the woman."

"And?"

"She didn't answer. She just took off. I tried to follow her, but — " She looked around again. "I'd bet anything that was her. But why would she take off like that?"

I could tell how disappointed she was that the girl had got away from her, so I tried to be positive.

"The important thing is that we found her, right?" I said.

"Yeah," Rebecca said, not nearly so positive. "But now what do we do?"

CHAPTER EIGHT

What we decided was that I would talk to Riel when we got back to school. But the funeral had gone on longer than we expected and then we hung around the church, watching people. Because of that, we got back to school just as the bell rang. I didn't have time to check in with Riel. As it was, I barely made it to my English class.

Ms Stephenson had been pushing us hard on writing skills ever since Christmas. She started every class by making us do what she called free writing. How it worked was that she wrote a word on the blackboard and then said, Go. We all had to write, not stopping for anything, until she said, Stop, ten minutes later. She said it didn't matter what we wrote — we could sit there writing *I don't know what to write* over and over again, but we had to keep writing. She said if we kept going, we'd be surprised. She said we'd always end up with something and that some of it might even be good. At first I hated it. Now I kind of enjoyed it. Sometimes I wrote things that weren't half bad.

We all had our heads down and we were all free writing — the word of the day was "love" and I was on a roll, mostly describing what it was like to hang out with Rebecca (Ms Stephenson said whatever we wrote was our business and that we didn't have to hand it in and we would never have to read it out) — when I realized that everyone around me was whispering. I looked up and almost had a heart attack. Looking in through the window in the classroom door, looking right at *me,* was Detective Canton. There was a uniformed cop with him, which, I think, was what had got everyone else's attention. He was looking at me, too, which made everyone in the classroom turn in my direction. I knew exactly what everyone was thinking: Oh boy, the cops are after Mike McGill again. I held my breath and hoped that they would go away.

They didn't.

The classroom door opened. Ms Stephenson, who had been marking assignments at her desk while we wrote, looked up. Ms Rather, the school principal, came into the room. Detective Canton stood in the doorway. He was still looking at me, which was making me nervous enough. I felt even worse when I saw Riel standing behind him, looking grim.

"Mike," Ms Rather said, "would you come with me, please."

Every eye in the class was on me as I stood up.

"Better bring your things with you, Mike," Ms Rather said.

I fumbled with my binder and my textbook. My legs felt wobbly as I followed her out of the classroom. I looked at Riel. He waited until Ms Rather had closed the classroom door behind her before he said, "Detective Canton wants to ask you a few questions, Mike." It was all he said. We all went down to the second floor where Riel said we could talk in his classroom. We went inside and Riel closed the door. Ms Rather didn't come in with us. She left it to Riel.

"Sit down, Mike," Detective Canton said.

I glanced at Riel again. He nodded. I sat.

"Is something wrong?" I said.

"Detective Canton wants to ask you some questions about Sal," Riel said. "I think you should answer them."

"Sal? What about him?" I said. I'm pretty sure my voice was shaking. I know my knees were. I was glad I was sitting down. A homicide detective wanted to ask me some questions about Sal. That wasn't good — for me or for Sal. "Did something happen to Sal?"

"He's in the hospital," Riel said.

"The hospital? Is he okay?"

"Someone beat him up pretty badly last night around eleven," Detective Canton said. "John tells me that you were home when it happened." I glanced at Riel. That was why he had said I should answer the questions, because he had looked in on me just before eleven. He knew that I hadn't done anything. He had seen me at home with his own eyes. "Do you know anything about it?" Detective Canton said.

Me?

"No," I said. "Sal's my friend."

"Sal said that two guys beat him up. He says they told him that if he knew what was good for him, he'd better not say anything about what happened at the convenience store," Detective Canton said.

"But he already told you everything he saw."

Detective Canton just looked at me.

I glanced at Riel. "Is Sal okay?"

Detective Canton was the one who answered. He said, "They kicked him pretty good. Cracked one of his ribs. He's lucky they didn't break it. Gave him a concussion, too. They're keeping him in the hospital for observation until at least tomorrow." He stared hard at me. "Are you sure you don't know anything about it, Mike?"

"No." Why did he keep asking me that? "I was at home. Besides, I'd never hurt Sal."

"I know you didn't do it," Detective Canton said. Maybe it was just my imagination, but he sounded a little disappointed that he couldn't nail me for that. "But when you went to see Vincent the other day, did he say anything that gave you the impression he and his buddies were planning to go after Sal?"

"No. No way." Wait a minute. Was he trying to trip me up again? "And anyway, I already told you that Vin doesn't know the two guys from the store. Besides, what good would it do Vin if Sal got beat up? Vin already said he was in the store. And Sal already told you he saw him."

"Maybe Vincent's friends are trying to help him," Detective Canton said. "Maybe they want Sal to lose his memory about what he saw. That happens sometimes, Mike. Suddenly a witness isn't one hundred percent sure he saw what he said he saw. He doesn't come right out and say he didn't see it.

Instead, he says he has doubts. So sure, maybe Sal saw Vincent come out of the store. But maybe, now that he thinks about it, Vincent didn't come out right after the other two guys. Maybe he came out a minute or two later. Or maybe now Sal's not sure which direction Vincent went in. Maybe it wasn't the same direction as the other two guys. Or maybe he suddenly remembers that he saw the two guys drop something. And, who knows, it could have been some of the money they stole. That would line up with what Vincent is saying — that all he did was pick up money that someone else had dropped. The defence would love it. It creates reasonable doubt. All we have is one eyewitness and now that eyewitness is having doubts about what really happened. You know what I mean, Mike?"

Cops. They looked at the dark side of every situation. They always came up with ways people could be scamming them. What a way to go through life.

"Sal told us he can't identify the guys who beat him up. It could have been the other guys from the convenience store. It could have been friends of theirs and Vincent's." There he was, lumping Vin in with them again. "One of them spoke to Sal, but Sal says he didn't recognize the voice." Detective Canton paused to look at me. "The thing is, Mike, they were waiting for Sal in the alley right next to the apartment building where he lives. So it raises the question: If he doesn't know them, how did they know where to find him?"

"You're saying Vin told them?" No way. "Vin doesn't know those guys," I said — *again*. "Vin didn't do anything. Why would he want to get Sal beat up if he didn't do anything?"

Detective Canton just shrugged. "Makes you wonder," he said. "At least, it sure makes *me* wonder. How do a couple of complete strangers know where to wait for Sal? But a friend — even an ex-friend — that's another story. Someone who knows Sal would know where to find him. You sure Vincent didn't say anything to you about getting even with Sal or maybe wanting to scare him?"

"The only thing he said was to tell Sal he didn't do it."

Detective Canton stared at me. Then he said, "By the way, Mike, we put out the robbery on Crime Stoppers. It'll be in the paper and on local TV. Who knows, maybe we'll get some tips."

What did he expect me to say to that?

"I hope it helps," I said.

Detective Canton looked at me a little while longer. Finally he thanked me for my time and left. After he'd gone, Riel said, "He's just doing his job, Mike."

Right.

"If you want me to," Riel said, "I'll run you over to the hospital after school. You can see how Sal is."

I told him no. I said I could get there on my own.

Then he said, "So, how was the funeral?"

The way I had it pictured in my head, it would go sort of like this:

Me: I saw the girl Vin told me about. She was at the funeral, but she got away before I could find out her name. You got any idea how I can track her down?

Riel: Tell me what she looks like and what she was wearing.

Me: (Here I give Riel her description.)

Riel (reaching for the phone): Let's call Canton and Mancini. They'll find her. Good work, Mike.

What actually happened:

I said, "I saw the girl Vin told me about. She was at the funeral, but she got away before I could find out her name. You got any idea how I can track her down?"

"What girl?" Riel said. He had sat down at his desk and was reaching for a stack of what looked like test papers.

"Vin said there was a girl in the store, remember?"

"Right." He didn't roll his eyes, but I could tell from his tone of voice that he probably wanted to. Mostly Riel is an okay guy, but sometimes he gets impatient, usually when he thinks someone is doing something stupid and they should know better. This was one of those times. The stupid things I was doing: believing Vin and wasting my time trying to prove he hadn't been lying to me.

"Vin described the girl to me," I said. "Short, spiky black hair, an eyebrow ring, with that tattoo Vin drew for me."

Riel looked up from the test papers, which was

how I knew he was interested. "And you saw this girl?"

I nodded.

"Where?"

"At the funeral."

He gave me a look like it was all falling into place. So *that* was why I'd gone to the funeral.

"You saw a girl with short, spiky black hair, an eyebrow ring, and a spider tattoo at the funeral?" he said.

"Well, actually, her hair was blond."

"But you just said — "

"Rebecca says she must have dyed her hair."

"So she had spiky *blond* hair?"

"Well, it wasn't spiky," I said. "It was a funeral. Rebecca says she probably wanted to look more normal."

"Rebecca?" Riel said, like he couldn't figure out why her name kept coming up. "Rebecca saw this girl?"

"I told you she was going to the funeral with me. Rebecca's the one who spotted her."

"Oh," Riel said. "So Rebecca has seen this girl before?"

"Not that I know of. But she noticed that this girl had a little scar over her eyebrow, like maybe it had been pierced."

Riel frowned. "So this blond girl you saw at the funeral wasn't wearing an eyebrow ring?"

"No, but — "

"But she had a little scar that *maybe* could have

been a piercing — " I never should have said *maybe*. " — according to Rebecca, who has never laid eyes on this girl before." He squinted into space. I couldn't tell if he was really trying to picture it or if he was just needling me. "But you saw the tattoo, right?" Riel said. "And it matched the picture Vin drew for you."

"Well, not exactly."

"Not exactly? Either it matched or it didn't, Mike."

"I didn't see it. She was wearing long sleeves."

"Let me get this straight," Riel said. I hate it when he says that, because it usually means he's going to lay out for me exactly how stupid I sound. "You saw a blond girl with non-spiky hair, no eyebrow ring and no tattoo, at least none that was visible, and, even though you personally have never seen this girl before, you think that she's the girl with black spiky hair, an eyebrow ring, and a spider tattoo that Vin *says* he saw in the store when that woman was shot." The way he said that one word, *says,* told me everything I needed to know about where this conversation was going. "Does that make sense even to you, Mike?"

"Well — "

"Because it doesn't add up for me. Look, I know you think Vin is your friend."

Think? "He *is* my friend," I said.

Riel shook his head. "After what happened last year, I thought maybe he'd learned his lesson. But it doesn't look like it, does it, Mike? If anything, it looks like he's got himself in an even bigger jam. If he keeps this up, he's going to be spending more time inside than he is outside."

"Yeah, but — "

"I'm not finished, Mike."

Right.

"You're doing great. I think you know that. Your grades have improved. They like you down at the community centre. All I hear is good things about you. You've got a nice girlfriend. You keep going the way you are, and I can see you in college in a couple of years. Maybe even university. You can do whatever you want with your life, Mike. And you know why? Because so far you've been making the right decisions, not the wrong ones, like Vin. It'd be nice if you could keep it that way, don't you think?"

"But what if Vin's telling the truth?" I said. "What if there really was a girl in the store and what if she could tell the cops that he didn't do anything?"

Riel looked at me as if he thought I was saying I could fly to the moon if I just flapped my arms hard enough.

"Vin was in the store," he said. "He ran out right after those other two guys and after those people were shot. He hid out from the police. When he was arrested, he had some of the stolen money on him. That paints a picture for me, Mike, and, to be honest, I can't understand why it doesn't paint the same picture for you."

I was actually grateful when the bell rang.

It turned out that the whole school had heard about what happened to Sal — except Rebecca and me, and that was because we'd gone to the funeral. At first I couldn't figure out how the news about Sal had got around so fast. Then I remembered Imogen. She was like CNN. She had broadcast all the news on Vin. Now she'd moved on to a new story — Sal.

"Are you going to see him?" Rebecca asked me. She was waiting for me at my locker after school.

"Yeah," I said. He was my friend, too, even if we hadn't been getting along all that great lately and even if he didn't think he was my friend. I thought about what he had said last time we talked — how he always felt like a third wheel on a two-wheel bike when he was around me and Vin. That sounded more like something a girl would say than something Sal would say. I was willing to bet Imogen had something to do with that, too.

"I'm coming with you," Rebecca said. When I gave her a look, she said, "I like Sal, too. Everybody likes Sal."

She dragged me into 7–Eleven on the way. She headed straight for the magazine rack and reached for a magazine that I had never heard of and never read. It was all about the outdoors — hiking and mountain climbing and deep-sea diving, that kind of thing.

"You planning to climb Everest?" I said.

"It's for Sal."

"Is Sal planning to climb Everest and somebody forgot to tell me?" I was kidding around, but Rebecca didn't even smile.

"It's Sal's big dream," she said. "Not climbing Everest. But getting away. Imogen says he talks about it all the time. What he really wants to do is backpack around the world. You know, like that English woman who walked all the way around the world." I'd never heard of that woman. "Sal wants to do something like that."

"He does?" Boy, that was news to me.

"According to Imogen," Rebecca said.

"How come I never heard about that?"

Rebecca just shrugged. I followed her up to the counter to pay for the magazine. It really bothered me — how come I didn't know about Sal's big dream? How come Sal had never mentioned it to me? It made me think. Things had changed a lot since I went to live with Riel. I had less time to hang out — Riel made sure of that. I paid more attention to my homework. I had a part-time job. And, for the past couple of months, I'd been spending more time with Rebecca than with almost anyone else.

Things had changed a lot more for Sal. His father was sick, which meant that Sal had to put in way more hours working than I did. He took his schoolwork more seriously than I did — without anyone pushing him. We didn't hang out as much as we used to. I watched Rebecca fish her wallet out of her purse and scrambled in my pocket for some money to give her. She waved it away with a smile.

"Sal's my friend, too," she said.

That's when it hit me — what the biggest change had been. Sal and I both had girlfriends now. I had Rebecca and he had Imogen. I spent a lot of time with Rebecca. I talked to her — girls like to talk. I told her stuff that I would never tell Sal, mostly because he'd probably think it was sappy. Rebecca never thought anything was sappy. Sal probably talked to Imogen. He probably told her things he didn't tell other people. He'd told her about his big dream. He'd told her how he felt about what had happened in the convenience store. Who knew what else he had told her?

* * *

Sal was sharing a hospital room with a really old guy who was either asleep or maybe in a coma, it was hard to tell which. We had to go past the old guy to get to Sal and the guy never moved, not even when I knocked into a chair near the end of his bed, and its feet made a loud scraping noise.

Sal was lying in his bed, which was rolled up a little at the head. His eyes were closed, even though Imogen was sitting on a chair beside him. She was holding his hand. I had never seen a girl holding Sal's hand before. It was a whole different way of looking at him.

Imogen didn't smile when she saw me. She said Sal's name in a soft voice, and Sal opened his eyes. He had some bad bruises on his face and a big cut on his lip that looked painful. There was a bandage on his right hand and more bruises on his arm. Detective Canton hadn't been kidding. He had been badly beaten.

Sal looked at Rebecca, who asked him how he was feeling and gave him the magazine. He smiled when he saw what it was — but it was a crooked kind of smile, like he was trying not to move the part of his lip that was cut. He thanked her. He looked at me, too, but just for a second. Then he turned away, which was how I knew that he was still mad at me. Part of me wanted to walk out of the room. I mean, what was the point of being there if he wouldn't even look at me, never mind talk to me? But I stayed, mostly because of what Rebecca would have thought if I left.

I walked around to the other side of the bed where he was looking.

"Hey, Sal," I said. "I heard what happened."

He didn't turn away from me this time. He looked right at me and said, "Yeah, I bet you did."

What was that supposed to mean?

"The cops talked to me," I said.

That got his interest. "Yeah?" he said.

"They thought Vin must have told those two guys about you — you know, your name and where they could find you."

"Right," Sal said. "*Vin.*" He put a spin on Vin's name, but I couldn't figure out why.

"I told them that couldn't be it," I said. "Vin doesn't know the two guys who were in the store, so he couldn't tell them anything."

"Right," Sal said again. It was turning out to be his favourite word. I was starting to get angry.

"Geeze, Sal, I already told you — "

"Hey, Mike," Rebecca said softly. Her message: *Calm down. Take it easy.*

"I never talked to Vin after he got arrested that time. I never went to see him when he was locked up," Sal said. "And you told me you didn't go and see him either."

"I didn't."

"I didn't go this time, either," Sal said.

Oh. He'd heard about my visit to Vin — maybe the cops had told him.

"I haven't seen him or spoken to him since last fall. So I never told him what happened with my dad," Sal said, his voice a perfect match to his hard, cold eyes. "I never told him that my dad lost his job and that my mother had to sell the house. I never told him that we had to move in with my mother's sister. I never told him my aunt's last name. My mom didn't tell anyone, either. She was too embarrassed."

He was practically yelling the words at me now. I wondered if he'd managed to wake up the old guy in the next bed, but I couldn't tell because of the curtain between Sal's side of the room and the old guy's side.

"So, Mike, how did those two guys that Vin doesn't know — that he just happened to be in the store with when it got robbed and then just happened to run out of the store after — how did they know where to find me? Vin didn't even know where to find me — unless someone told him." His eyes were directly on mine now. I think if he hadn't been so badly beat up, he would have been all over me, trying to hurt me.

"You think *I* had something to do with it?" I said.

"You went to see Vin," Sal said. "Because he's such a good friend of yours, is that it? Because you've known him forever. Isn't that what you said? You've known him since kindergarten. Me you've only known since fourth grade. How long you know a person, that's the most important thing to you, right, Mike? Not whether that person is honest or a liar, not whether that person does the right thing or the wrong thing, right?"

"I never said anything to Vin about you," I said. "And he never asked." What was that I saw in his eyes? Not anger this time — at least, not for that split second. No, it was more like he was hurt. Hurt that Vin hadn't asked about him. "If he knows where you live now, he didn't find out from me."

The two girls were silent. Imogen was staring at me like she wished I'd crawl into the nearest garbage can where I belonged. Rebecca was looking watery-eyed at Sal, like she felt sorry for him.

"My mother wants me to stay out of it," Sal said. "She doesn't want me to talk to the police anymore. She doesn't want me to testify at the trial. She's afraid if I do, those two guys will kill me. I'm not kidding, Mike. That's what she said to me. *Stay out of it or they'll kill you.* She thinks it's like that here.

She doesn't trust the cops, Mike. Not after what happened back home and for sure not after what happened to my dad." Sal's father had been tortured before Sal's family fled Guatemala. And last fall, when Sal's father had a breakdown and was acting violent one night, it looked for a while like the cops were going to shoot him. I couldn't blame Sal's mother for how she felt. But Sal — that was another story.

"And the whole reason I'm in this position," he said, "not just in this bed, but in this position with the cops telling me what I should do and my mother telling me what I should do, both of them saying different things — is because of Vin."

"He swears he didn't rob that store," I said. I was looking at Sal, but I saw Imogen out of the corner of my eye. I bet the minute she left the hospital, she'd be telling everyone all about Sal's disloyal so-called friend Mike McGill.

"I have a cracked rib," Sal said.

"I heard."

"The doctor here says I have to rest. He says I should stay home from school for a few days." He opened his eyes and I saw that there were tears in them. Imogen squeezed the hand that wasn't bandaged. "He said for sure I wouldn't be able to work for a while. You know what that's going to mean for my family, Mike? They need me to be working."

I didn't know what to say.

CHAPTER NINE

Imogen was still holding Sal's hand. I guess I was glad about that. I was glad that Sal had someone he could talk to, someone who seemed to care about him the way Rebecca cared about me. Rebecca took my hand. She told Sal she hoped he would get out of the hospital soon. She said that if he wanted her to, she would lend him her notes from history class. Rebecca and Sal were both in Riel's class. I used to be, too, but Ms Rather transferred me out when I started living with Riel. Imogen told Rebecca it was okay, she had a *friend* in the class who was going to photocopy her notes for Sal. Rebecca flinched when Imogen said that — I think it was the way she said it that bothered Rebecca. Then Sal said, "Thanks, Rebecca. I appreciate the offer. Really." He was showing me that he didn't blame Rebecca for anything, not even for sticking with me. He was showing us all what a great guy he was.

As we were walking out of the room, I heard Imogen say, "You should stay away from him, Sal. He's bad news. Just listen to him — he still believes Vin, not you. He's on Vin's side."

I glanced at Rebecca to see if she had heard. She tightened her grip on my hand, but she didn't say anything. We left the hospital.

Rebecca wanted to stop for coffee on the way home. There was a place on Danforth that she liked, a little café where you could get latte that comes in great big bowls. Rebecca ordered that. I ordered hot chocolate. We sat near the window and Rebecca stared through the glass while she sipped her coffee. She didn't say anything for the longest time. Then she closed her eyes.

I'd been thinking about what Sal had said — about guys waiting for him at his house. If you ask me, he'd made the case that Vin couldn't have had anything to do with it. First of all — and, boy, I was getting tired of pointing it out to everyone — Vin said he didn't know the guys who had robbed the store. Second, as far as I knew, even if Vin knew that Sal had moved (and I wasn't sure he did), he didn't know *where* Sal lived. So how could he have told two guys where to wait for Sal to beat him up? The thing that killed me was that Sal thought he had the answer to that — *I'd* told Vin. Geeze, it was like he thought I was in it with Vin. I glanced at Rebecca. I wondered what she was thinking about. I wondered what she thought about what Sal had said.

"Rebecca?" I said.

"Mmmm?" Her eyes were still closed, like maybe she didn't want to look at me anymore.

"Rebecca, are you okay?"

"I'm visualizing."

"Visualizing what?" Maybe visualizing life without me.

"You know sometimes when someone asks you a person's name — a movie star or something, you know, What's the name of that guy who was in that movie with Tom Cruise? And you know you know the guy's name, but you can't think of it — and then it comes to you at four in the morning. It's been rattling around in the back of your brain for hours and hours, but it's only when you're not thinking about it that, *pop,* all of a sudden there it is, the guy's name, flashing in your brain like a neon sign."

"Uh-huh," I said slowly. What was she talking about?

"I'm visualizing that girl."

"The girl from the store?"

"The girl from the funeral. I've been trying to clear my brain so that maybe I could see something about her that would help us. What did you think I was thinking about, Mike? Dumping you?" She opened her eyes and smiled at me. When Rebecca smiles, it's like the whole world is clear blue skies and sweet, warm sunshine.

"So," I said, "did you see any visions?"

"Bright orange."

"Orange?"

She nodded. "That girl we saw at the funeral. She had a bright orange shirt or something in her bag. Did you notice?"

I shook my head.

"Well, I did."

"Rebecca," I said, keeping my voice soft and gentle so that she wouldn't think I was criticizing, "I bet there must be a million people in the city who have orange shirts."

"It had a nametag on it."

"*What?*" Okay, now *that* was useful information. "What was the name on it?"

"When I close my eyes I see bright orange and I see the corner of something square with a pin on the back of it, like a nametag."

First it was a nametag. Now it was *like* a nametag. I was starting to understand how I must have sounded to Riel.

"So you're not sure it was a nametag?" I said, trying to be careful that I didn't come across like I doubted her or was being negative.

"I'm sure it was a nametag, Mike. I just couldn't see the front of it." She turned her brown eyes on me full force. "She has a job, Mike. She works someplace where she has to wear a bright orange T-shirt."

There are more than two million people living in Toronto and who knows how many businesses.

"I know what you're thinking," Rebecca said. "Where? Where does she work?" She shook her head. "I'm sure of what I saw, but I'm not psychic." She picked up her great big bowl of latte and took a sip. She was quiet while she finished it and then she was quiet all the way home.

* * *

Susan was at the house when I got back from the hospital. She was sitting on the sofa in the living room, not doing anything, which was unusual. Usually she was either reading or she had her binder open and was going over wedding details.

Today she just looked tense. I wondered why. I thought about Riel and his secret conversations and meetings with the mysterious Kate.

"Mike," she said, standing up all of a sudden when I came into the room.

Riel appeared in the door to the kitchen. He was wearing an apron and had a wooden spoon in one hand.

"Did you see Sal?" he said.

"Yeah."

"How is he?"

"He's not going to be able to work for a while."

"That's going to be tough on his family, isn't it?"

"Yeah."

Riel was silent for a moment. Then he and Susan looked at each other. Susan seemed even tenser now. All I could think was: oh-oh.

"What's wrong?" I said.

"I'm afraid Susan has some bad news, Mike," Riel said. "Well, maybe that's overstating it. Maybe it won't matter."

I glanced at Susan. She shook her head.

"I'm so sorry, Mike," she said.

Sorry? It didn't sound good.

"Sorry about what?" I said.

Susan reached into the big purse she usually carried. It was on the floor at her feet. "About the videotape you made me," she said, pulling out a videocassette and handing it to me. "I lent it to Trish. She watched it. She enjoyed it, Mike. She said to thank you." I looked at the cassette as I took it from her. It had a label on it now and a name I didn't recognize — Jeremy. "The thing is, Mike — " She glanced at Riel.

"It got taped over," Riel said.

"Taped over?"

"Trish's son taped over it," Susan said. Her voice was as shaky as her smile.

"It was an accident," Riel said. "But, like I said, it's probably no big deal. You were home that night. You had nothing to do with that robbery. I don't think you have anything to worry about."

I glanced at Susan again. I wished she looked as confident as Riel was trying to sound.

"I'm sorry, Mike," she said again.

"It's okay. It's not your fault."

Riel was still standing in the doorway to the kitchen. He studied me, as if he were trying to decide something. Then he dropped another bomb on me.

"Vin's mother called," he said.

I hadn't spoken to Vin's mother since last fall. One time I stopped in at a grocery store to pick up some things that Riel said we needed and I had seen her across the store in another aisle. I got out of there fast. It was lame, I know. I mean, I had known her as long as I had known Vin, which was practically my whole life. I should have gone to talk to her. But I didn't know what to say.

"Did she want to talk to me?" I said. I hoped she didn't. I still wouldn't know what to say.

"She wants you to call Vin." That explained the

look on Riel's face. "She said she saw him today and he asked her to ask you if you could call him." He fished into his pocket and pulled out a slip of paper. "If you decide to do it, this is the number. You call and identify yourself. You're on the list."

"What list?"

"Vin's not allowed to get phone calls from just anybody. His parents can call. His lawyer can call. Anyone else has to be approved. His mother got you approved."

"But you said I should stay away from Vin," I said.

"I gave you some advice. I still think it's good advice, but you have to make your own decisions." He handed me the slip of paper. "Supper's going to be a while." He went back into the kitchen.

I stared at the phone number. What did Vin want to talk to me about? Should I call him? If I did, would the cops find out?

"John's making mushroom risotto," Susan said. I'd almost forgotten she was there. "You like risotto, Mike?"

I told her I didn't think I'd ever tasted it.

"Well, then, you're in for a treat." She looked at the piece of paper I was still holding. "Are you going to call your friend?"

Friend.

I stuck the piece of paper into my pocket. "Maybe later," I said.

Maybe.

"I really am sorry, Mike," she said again.

"It's okay," I told her. "Really. John's right. I mean, I didn't *do* anything."

"Of course he's right," she said. She patted the sofa cushion next to the one she was sitting on. "Come here. Let's look at tuxedos while John makes dinner."

Tuxedos?

"Me?"

"You're in the wedding party, Mike," she said. "You need to wear a tuxedo."

Wait a minute. "I'm in the wedding party?"

She looked surprised.

"John didn't talk to you about it?"

"No."

She sighed. For a minute I thought she was going to get mad. But she didn't.

"Trust me," she said. "You're going to need a tuxedo. Sit down. I'll show you what you can choose from." She reached for some wedding magazines.

A tuxedo is basically a suit. Sure, it's a fancy suit that you wear on special occasions. But it's a suit, so I thought, what's the big deal? Except, like everything else to do with the wedding, it turned out there were tons of choices. There were different colours, for one thing, even different colours of black. There were different cuts. There were different jackets — some that looked like regular suit jackets, others that were longer, and still others that were short in front and long in the back, like the kind of thing you'd see on an English butler in some old movie. Boy, and there were different lapels — wide, narrow, in-between — and different kinds of shirts you would wear.

"What did John choose?" I said. He probably knew way more about tuxedos than I did.

"We haven't discussed it yet," Susan said. "You pick out a couple that you like, then I'll talk to him and you can go and try some on, and hopefully we can get that nailed down." The wedding was less than six weeks away. Susan was talking a lot these days about nailing things down. "What about this?" she said, pointing to a black tuxedo with a long jacket. "I think you'd look handsome in that, Mike. I bet Rebecca would think so, too."

"Yeah?" I couldn't picture it. I had some nice pants and a jacket that Riel had bought me and that I had worn a couple of times when I'd had to meet a lawyer or a probation officer or when I went to see my caseworker. But a tuxedo?

Susan smiled. "Yeah," she said. "I've never met a man — short man, fat man, bald man, tall man — who didn't look terrific in a tuxedo. And you're a good-looking guy, Mike. Which means that you'll look incredible in a tux."

"Yeah?" She thought I was good-looking?

"Definitely," she said.

"Mike, come and set the table," Riel called from the kitchen.

Susan reached for her wedding binder, pulled a little pad of sticky notes from the flap inside the cover, and stuck a note on the magazine page. "I'll show it to John later."

Mushroom risotto was okay, but I didn't go ga-ga over it the way Susan did. After we ate, Susan said that she had to go. She had a friend who made cakes and pastries. The friend was designing the wedding cake. I'd never heard of a cake being designed before. Riel said he had some prep to do and that he'd talk to her later. I was on clean-up detail. I had almost finished when Riel called me to the phone.

"It's Rebecca," he said. He had his hand over the mouthpiece as he handed me the receiver. "She sounds nervous. She sounds nervous every time I talk to her. Do me a favour, Mike? Tell her I don't bite." He went into the living room.

"I had to go to the video store right after I got home, to return a movie," she said. She didn't sound nervous to me. She sounded breathless, like she had just run all the way home.

"Yeah?" I said.

"I went to that one on Danforth. You know, the one that's on the way to school."

"Yeah," I said. It was the one I always went to because it was also the closest one to Riel's house, only from a different direction. "But I thought you didn't go there. I thought you went to the other place, you know, because of all those gift certifi-cates." A friend of Rebecca's family was assistant manager of a store in a different video chain. She'd given Rebecca a whole wad of gift certificates for Christmas. The only downside was that the other video store was a lot farther from Rebecca's house.

She had to get a drive to go there.

"I do," she said. "But my mom wanted to show a movie to one of her classes and they didn't have it there, so she rented it from the store on Danforth. And I just returned it for her. You've seen the shirts they wear at that store, haven't you, Mike? You know what colour they are?"

"Yeah," I said. "They're red."

"They *were* red," she said. Her voice was high and squeaky, which told me she was excited about something. "They're doing this special promotion. And because of that, everyone who works in the store is wearing a bright orange T-shirt instead of the regular red ones. They've been wearing them for a couple of weeks now."

Bright orange.

"You mean, like the T-shirt you saw in the girl's bag."

"Exactly," Rebecca said. "They also wear name-tags. Square ones, just like I told you. I bet she works at one of those video stores."

"I guess she doesn't work at the one you were in, huh?" I said.

"I asked." I wondered how she had put the question, considering she didn't know the girl's name. "She doesn't work there. But there are three other stores in the area, Mike, and one of them is almost brand new. It's been open less than a month." Her voice was squeaky again, like a mouse. "We should check them out. We could go now if you want. They're open until midnight."

I glanced at the clock on the stove. It was eight o'clock and I hadn't done my homework. I hadn't done anything about Vin either.

"I can't," I said. I felt like a little kid.

"How about last period tomorrow?" she said. We both had a spare.

"Okay. But I'm working tomorrow night, so I have to watch the time."

After I hung up, I finished cleaning up the kitchen. Then I fished the piece of paper with Vin's phone number out of my pocket. I wondered what he wanted. There was only one way to find out. I picked up the phone and took it into the living room.

"Is it okay if I take the phone upstairs to make a call?" I said.

Riel looked up from the magazine. "You going to call Vin?"

I nodded.

"Bring it down again when you're finished," Riel said.

* * *

I went up to my room and closed the door. My hands were shaking so bad you'd have thought I was calling a girl I had just met instead of a guy I had known all my life. The woman who answered on the other end asked me for my name. She told me to hold. A minute passed. Then another and another. I was wondering if she had forgotten about me. Finally:

"Hello?"

124

"Vin, it's me. Mike."

"Hey, Mike." He sounded tired. Or maybe he was just down. I bet it was no fun being locked up.

"I got a message you wanted to talk to me."

"Yeah," Vin said. "I was wondering if you were having any luck with what we talked about."

"About the girl, you mean?"

"About what we talked about," Vin said. His voice was funny. I got the idea he was being careful. Maybe they listened in on phone calls. Or maybe there was someone nearby he didn't want to hear.

"I haven't found . . . I haven't come through yet," I said. "But I have an idea I'm going to follow up on tomorrow."

"Yeah?" All of a sudden he sounded a lot brighter. "You think you're going to be able to do it?"

"I don't know, Vin. But I'm trying."

"That's great, Mike. I really appreciate it."

"Vin, did you hear what happened to Sal?"

He hadn't, so I filled him in.

"You didn't talk to anyone about him, did you, Vin?" I said.

"What do you mean?"

"Sal said the guys who beat him up warned him not to say anything about what he saw at the store. So he thinks you must have given someone his name or told them where to find him." I didn't mention that Sal had moved. I wanted to hear Vin's reaction first.

"Me?" Vin said. "Hey, give me a break, Mike. All I want is to get out of here. And right now the only way I can see that happening is if you do what we talked about."

"Or if Sal all of a sudden isn't sure what he saw," I said.

"Right," Vin said. "Like that's going to happen. He gave me up pretty fast, Mike. He isn't going to change his story. Not Sal." Vin knew Sal as well as I did. If he was disappointed by Sal's stubbornness, he sure didn't show it. "I can't get a lot of phone calls, Mike. So do me a favour? If you find out anything, can you give a note to my mother? She's come every day so far."

"Does she still cry?"

"Yeah, but usually only when she first sees me and then again when she has to leave. The rest of the time she's pretty normal."

"What about your dad?"

"He's only been here once. My mom keeps making excuses for him."

There wasn't much else to say, so I told him I'd do what I could and then I hung up. I was on my way back down to the living room with the phone when it rang. It was a woman. She asked to speak to Riel. I went downstairs and handed the phone to him. He said, "Hello? Kate, hi." A moment later he said, "Now?" sounding surprised. "Oh. Okay. Sure." When he hung up, he said, "I have to go out for a little while, Mike."

Out to see Kate.

"What about Susan?" I said.

"What about her?"

"What should I tell her?"

"You don't have to tell her anything, Mike. She's not coming back here tonight. She's staying at her place."

Oh.

"You two are still getting married, aren't you?" I said.

Riel gave me a look, but he didn't answer.

"Do your homework," he said instead.

Right.

CHAPTER TEN

The next day, there were all kinds of rumours going around school. Like this one: "Hey, McGill, is it true Vin paid to have Sal beat up?" And this one: "Hey, Mike, I heard you told Vin's friends where they could find Sal." And this one, which Rebecca told me. "Hillary Whalen is telling everyone that Imogen told her that the cops questioned you about where you were the night the store was robbed and that you told them you were home alone. Imogen is saying that she wouldn't be surprised to find out that you lied to the police and that you were one of the guys who was in the store with Vin. According to Hillary, Imogen is also saying that she's pretty sure that Sal suspects it, too, but that he didn't see you so he hasn't said anything to the police. She's saying that she thinks you had something to do with Sal being beaten up. In fact, according to Hillary, she's saying she wouldn't be surprised if you were one of the guys who actually did it."

"What?" Why would she say those things about me?

"If you ask me," Rebecca said, "Imogen's just mad at you because you believe Vin instead of Sal."

"It's not that I don't believe Sal," I said. "I know he saw what he saw. But he didn't see what happened inside the store. He just saw Vin come out. If he'd actually been in the store, if he'd actually seen what happened . . . "

"Seeing is believing, huh, Mike?" Rebecca said.

"Yeah," I said. If you see it, you believe it. But did it work the other way around? Was believing seeing? If you believed someone the way I believed Vin, did that mean you were seeing the truth? "I wasn't anywhere near that store. And I would never do anything to hurt Sal. Never."

"I know." Rebecca squeezed my arm. "Don't let it get to you, Mike. The people who matter believe you."

She meant that she believed me. I was pretty sure Riel did, too. But what about Sal? He mattered to me. What did he think?

* * *

Rebecca and I met behind the school on our spare. We walked to the subway station and took the train east. We got off and walked the three blocks to the first video store on Rebecca's list. Rebecca was moving fast, like she couldn't wait to get there. She was really pumped. I had to grab her to stop her from running right into the store.

"What are we going to say?" I asked.

"First we're going to see if she's there."

"Which she won't be."

"If she's there," Rebecca said, "we can talk to her."

"You already tried that. It didn't work."

"Last time, I only had a chance to ask her if she knew Mrs. Lee," Rebecca said. "This time we're going to be more direct — we're going to tell her that we know she was there. We're going to make sure she goes to the police."

"What if she's not there?"

"If she's not there, we ask if she works there."

But that was the thing. "How can we ask when we don't even know her name?"

Rebecca gave me a look. "You could at least *try* to think positive, Mike," she said.

"Sorry."

Rebecca opened the door and swept into the store ahead of me. When I followed her in I saw that she was right about the T-shirts. The store was busy — way busier than I would have expected for two-thirty on a Thursday afternoon. There were at least a dozen customers in the aisles, and just after we went in the store an electronic bell sounded as a couple more people came in. But still, you couldn't miss those T-shirts. They were the colour of orange Popsicles. Rebecca walked up and down the aisles, checking out everyone who was wearing one. Big surprise: the girl we had seen at the funeral wasn't one of them. But I didn't say anything.

Rebecca went up to the cash. I trailed after her and stood back a pace, pretending to look at the candy display. Maybe I wasn't convincing because a guy who was checking out the new DVDs for sale gave me a look. He kept right on looking at me after that. If he hadn't had the back and sides of his head shaved, I would have thought he was a security guard checking me out for shoplifting. Then I thought, Maybe they have undercover security. He was making me nervous, the way he was staring at me. I tried to stay casual as I focused on what Rebecca was saying.

"Excuse me," she said to the guy who was standing behind the cash, looking at a computer screen while he tapped the keys. He was maybe nineteen or twenty. I wondered if he worked there full time, you know, if this was his whole life, or if he was in school or something. He smiled automatically when he looked from the screen to Rebecca.

"How can I help you?" he said. He said it the way some people say, How are you?— not because they really want to know but because it's been drilled into their heads that that's what they're supposed to say.

"I was in here last week," Rebecca said. "I spoke to one of the other clerks."

"Sales associates," the guy said, correcting her.

Rebecca nodded. "We were talking about movies and she made some recommendations which — stupid me — I should have written them down. Anyway, I was wondering when she's going to be in because I'd love to talk to her again."

"What's her name?" the guy behind the cash said.

"I don't know," Rebecca said. She was looking at the nametag on the guy's shirt. "I guess I should have noticed, huh? But she has an eyebrow ring and black hair — at least it was black last week, but it was dyed, you know, and when we were talking she told me she was thinking of maybe going blond." She looked at the guy again. The T-shirts were short-sleeved. "And she had a tattoo on her left arm. A spider tattoo."

The guy was shaking his head. "Are you two sure

you were in this store?" he said.

"Yes. Why?"

"First of all, nobody but nobody is allowed to wear any jewellery on their face. Earrings, that's okay. You got your belly button pierced, that's your own business. But no eyebrow rings, no nose rings, no lip rings, no tongue studs. At least, not while you're on shift. And second, I've been working here for two years, and I've never seen anyone like the person you just described. There's never been a girl with a spider tattoo working here."

Rebecca had spoken softly — she always spoke softly except when she was excited — but this guy had a loud voice. I glanced around. A couple of other orange T-shirts were looking in our direction. So were a couple of customers, including the guy with the shaved head. He seemed really interested in what was going on. Or maybe he was just interested in Rebecca.

"Are you sure?" Rebecca said to the guy behind the counter. "Because I know I was talking to her."

"If you were talking to her in this store, then you were talking to her in your dreams," the guy said, impatient now. "Nobody like that works here."

Rebecca actually thanked him. I wouldn't have bothered. But I noticed that she wasn't quite as bouncy leaving the store as she had been going in.

"You didn't think we'd get that lucky, did you?" I said.

"No, I guess not," she said. But I could tell she'd been hoping.

"You said there's four stores in this area — this one, the one on the Danforth, and two more, right?" She nodded. "So, two down and two to go."

She smiled at me, I guess because I was trying to think positive.

We got back on the subway and went a little farther east. The third store was a lot like the one we'd just been in, but not as busy. There were maybe two customers inside and one more came in after us. There were only three bright orange T-shirts. Rebecca approached one of them, a girl this time, and launched into her pitch. The girl was shaking her head before Rebecca was even halfway through.

"Are you sure you have the right store?" she said. "Because no one like that works here."

Rebecca started to get discouraged.

"Besides the stores in this area, how many more stores do they have in the city?" I asked her after we were outside again.

"Fifteen," she said.

I was sorry I had asked. But I held her hand and said, "If we have to, we'll go to all of them."

The next store, the new one, turned out to be three times bigger than the other two and twice as hard to get to. First we had to take the subway. Then we had to ride a crowded bus. When we finally got there, we walked the aisles together, checking all the bright orange T-shirts. No girl.

"So?" I said. "Are you going to ask or what?"

Rebecca shook her head. "Why don't you do it this time?"

"Me? What would I say?"

"Say what I said."

I looked around. I'd been hoping that Rebecca would keep doing the talking. She was good at it — she was friendly and convincing. I was afraid I wouldn't pull it off.

"Ask her," Rebecca said, nudging me and nodding to a short, brown-skinned woman wearing an orange T-shirt. She looked a lot older than the rest of the clerks.

I took a deep breath and went over to her. Rebecca stayed where she was.

"Excuse me," I said.

"How can I help you?" she said, just like the guy behind the cash in the first store we'd gone to.

"I'm looking for a girl who works here," I said. "She's about this tall." I held my hand up to show where the top of her head would be if she were standing right beside me. "She usually wears an eyebrow ring when she's not working, so she has this little scar right here. She has a spider tattoo right here on her arm. And she has black hair. Short. She's pretty."

"You must mean Amanda," the woman said. "Except she changed her hair colour. She's a blonde now."

That had to be her.

"Yeah, Amanda. Is she working today?"

The woman shook her head.

"Do you know when she will be working?" I said.

"You have to talk to the shift supervisor," she

said. "She's up there." I looked in the direction she was pointing and saw a guy in a bright orange T-shirt behind the counter, and two women in bright orange T-shirts. One of them was restocking shelves. The other one was straightening the snack display.

"Who's the shift supervisor?" I said.

"Lorraine. She's the one in front of the snack counter."

"Thanks," I said.

Lorraine turned out to be young enough that she could have been the daughter of the woman I had just been talking to.

"Excuse me," I said.

"How may I help you?" Lorraine said, smiling at me, but not really smiling, if you know what I mean. It was more like a reflex. They really pounded it into their heads in these stores: smile, *smile,* SMILE. The bright orange shirt who had been restocking shelves walked to the back of the store. I saw her say something to the woman I had just been talking to.

"I was wondering if you could tell me when Amanda is working," I said.

Her smile vanished.

"Amanda is no longer with us," she said.

That figured. Nothing could ever be easy, right?

"Do you know how I can contact her?" I said.

She didn't ask me why I wanted to know. She didn't hesitate even a split second. She just said, "No."

"It's kind of important," I said.

An electronic bell sounded as two customers entered the store. Lorraine glanced at them, her eyes sharp as she checked them out. I wondered if she checked everyone out like that or if she saved it for customers who looked like those two — big guys, one with the hood of his sweatshirt pulled up so I couldn't see his face.

"I really need to get in touch with her," I said.

Lorraine turned back to me. "Sorry," she said, except that she didn't sound sorry. "Store policy. We don't give out information on employees."

"But you just said she doesn't work here anymore."

"Or former employees." She turned back to the snack display and plumped up a couple of bags of chips before setting them back carefully into the chip rack.

I turned to look at Rebecca.

The bright orange T-shirt who had been restocking the shelves breezed past Lorraine.

"Going on break," she said. The electronic bell sounded as she pushed her way out the door.

Rebecca and I left the store and stood outside, trying to decide what to do next. People went in, people came out. A pile of kids all of a sudden descended on the area. Some of the kids went into the video store, but most of them stayed outside. A couple of guys came out of the store, pushing their way through the kids who were outside horsing around and being really loud. Lorraine looked out at them. They were the same two guys she'd checked out on their way in. Then I saw that I'd been wrong — she wasn't looking at them. No, she was looking at the cop car that was pulling up to the curb outside the store. Seeing that car made me clench up — every time I ran into a cop, it was bad news. Rebecca must have noticed because she nudged me. There was a sign posted in the store window and another stuck in the window of the store next to it, one of those discount shoe places. The sign said: *Loitering will result in police being called.* I wondered if Lorraine had called the cops when the pack of kids had showed up. The kids didn't even seem to notice. The cops got out of the car. The two guys who had pushed through the kids and were standing a little farther down the curb turned suddenly and walked away, which made me think that maybe Lorraine had special radar, maybe she'd been working in the store long enough to know who to watch. The cops went up to the kids. One of them pointed out the sign. The kids groaned and made a lot of noise, but they got going. The cops got back in their car and sat there, watching. Rebecca and I started to move, too. That's when the orange T-shirt who was on break — on a smoke break, it turned out — said, "Why are you looking for Amanda?"

"What?" I turned around. She was standing out of range of the store windows.

"You were asking about Amanda. How come?" She blew some smoke in our direction. Rebecca waved it away with one hand.

"It's personal," I said. I wished the cops would go away. They were making me nervous.

The orange T-shirt snorted. "If it's personal, how come you had to ask Millie her name?"

I guessed Millie was the first woman I had spoken to. I glanced at Rebecca. She shook her head and said, "Go ahead and tell her."

Huh?

She shook her head again and looked at the bright orange T-shirt.

"The last time he was in here, he talked to her," she said. "And he really liked her. But he's also the biggest wuss on the planet. He was afraid to ask her for her name and number. So this time he dragged me along for moral support. He was going to ask her out." She gave me a withering look. "You know what Grandpa's always saying — you have to strike while the iron's hot."

"You two are related?" the bright orange T-shirt said.

"He's my brother," Rebecca said. Her voice was so full of contempt that I was glad I *wasn't* related to her. "You are *such* a loser," she said to me.

"You really are if you're interested in Amanda Brown," the bright orange T-shirt said, looking at me. "She got fired in record time — two weeks. I thought I'd never see her again. No such luck. She dropped by a couple of days ago and returned her T-shirts — as if anyone else is ever going to wear them." She looked me over. "You don't seriously

138

want to go out with her, do you?"

Rebecca shrugged. "What can I say?" she said to the bright orange T-shirt. "He really knows how to pick them."

"What was she fired for?" I asked.

"For being late — every day. Megan D. only hired her because a friend of hers recommended Amanda."

"Megan D.?" Rebecca said. I had a pretty good idea what she was thinking: maybe we should talk to this Megan D.

"There's three different Megans who work here," the bright orange T-shirt said. "Megan Doherty — Megan D. — is the store manager."

"Megan *Doherty?*" Rebecca said. She sounded surprised. "Thin, shoulder-length brown hair, dark brown eyes?"

The bright orange T-shirt nodded. "You know her?"

"I think she went to school with my sister," Rebecca said. Her cheeks flushed slightly. "With *our* sister." Rebecca had an older sister who lived in Vancouver. I'd never met her. "Except I thought she worked for your competition."

I stared at her.

"Yeah," the bright orange T-shirt said. "That's her. That's why they hired her — because she knows the competition. But she sure doesn't know trouble when she sees it. I could have told her Amanda wasn't going to work out. I got a vibe off her the first time I saw her. But Megan hired her anyway because a friend of hers asked her to. I was right. Amanda turned out to be a total disaster. Besides never getting to work on time, she was always screwing up the cash. Everyone complained about her. And she had weird hair, you know?" She made it sound like that was the worst thing. "Then Megan found out that she'd lied on her resumé. She had no choice — she had to fire her."

"So I guess Megan and her friend aren't friends anymore, huh?" Rebecca said.

"I'll say," the bright orange T-shirt said. "Megan's friend was killed last week. Shot to death in a convenience store. Do you believe it?" She took one last drag on her cigarette before throwing it down on the ground and crushing it out. "You got a pen?" she said.

Rebecca fumbled in her purse. I bet she was thinking what I was thinking: it was a small world.

"I meant him," the bright orange T-shirt said, nodding at me. "You still want to ask Amanda out?" I nodded. "I can give you her phone number."

Rebecca had found a pen and was scrambling for paper, but the bright orange T-shirt was already rattling it off, so Rebecca wrote the number on the back of her hand.

"Ask me how come I know her phone number by heart when I can't stand her," the bright orange T-shirt said. "Go ahead, ask me."

"Okay," I said. "How come?"

"Because, like I said, Amanda was late for work every single day that she worked here, and every time, Megan got me to call her and tell her to get her butt into the store or else. She would have fired anyone else after the first two warnings. But she kept getting me to call Amanda, kept giving her extra chances because Amanda was special, on account of Megan's friend." She sounded disgusted. "I gotta get back to work."

"Do you know where she lives?" Rebecca said.

The bright orange T-shirt shook her head. Rebecca jabbed me with her elbow and nodded at the T-shirt. Right.

"Thanks for the number," I said.

"Whatever," the bright orange T-shirt said.

Rebecca grinned at me.

"Now what?" I said.

"What do you think, Mike?"

CHAPTER ELEVEN

"But I don't want to phone her," I said. "I want to talk to her in person."

"Okay," Rebecca said. She was striding along slightly ahead of me, in a hurry to get somewhere, but I couldn't figure out where because we had no idea where Amanda Brown lived.

"Hey, wait," I said as we passed a phone booth. "Don't we want to look up her address?"

Rebecca looked first at me and then at the phone booth. "There's no phone book in there, as usual."

"Okay, so let's call Information."

"And ask them what?"

"Amanda Brown's address."

Rebecca gave me a funny look. "Do you have any idea how many Browns there are in the city, Mike?"

"Yeah, but how many Amanda Browns are there?"

"Or A. Browns," Rebecca said. "And that's assuming she has a phone listed under her name, not under one of her parents' names."

Right.

"So, you have a better idea?" I said.

"As a matter of fact, I do." She looped one arm through mine and we started walking again. Ten minutes later we were at the public library and using a computer to get onto the Internet. Rebecca typed in a URL that, it turned out, took us to the phone company's online directory.

"What about all those A. Browns?" I said.

Rebecca clicked on something, read the phone number on the back of her hand and typed it onto the screen. Then she clicked Search. A name and address popped up. Rebecca glanced at me while she wrote down the information.

"What's the matter, Mike?" she said. "You never used a reverse look-up before?"

Riel had a computer at home that he let me use. But, no, I had never used it to look up someone's address. Mostly I used it for homework, games and downloading music.

I looked at what Rebecca had written down: *T.C. Brown* and an address. I knew the street. It was located south of my school in a not-so-great neighbourhood.

"So, you want to go there?" Rebecca said.

"Now?"

I glanced at my watch. I had to be at work in exactly one hour. I was pretty sure I'd be able to make it.

"Okay," I said.

So that's what we did.

* * *

The street Amanda Brown lived on was even more run-down than I remembered. The reason I knew the street: my uncle Billy used to live there before he started to take care of me.

The houses were all small and semi-detached. They all looked shabby, but that was mostly because they had eavestroughs that sagged or they needed a fresh coat of paint or new windows. It looked like the people who lived there couldn't be bothered. Probably some of them couldn't, or the houses were owned by landlords who couldn't be bothered — that had been Billy's problem. But I bet some of them were owned by people who didn't have the extra money for a paint job or a whole new set of windows.

Amanda Brown's house was one of the most decrepit. The screen in the outside door was torn. The grey paint on the porch floor was mostly scuffed off. I glanced at Rebecca. She was staring at the house. I wondered if she'd ever been up close to one as run-down as this. Rebecca's parents were pretty well off. Rebecca's mother was an artist and an art teacher. Her father was a contractor. Not only was their house nice, it was pretty inside, with lots of bright colours and paintings.

"Ring the bell," Rebecca whispered.

There was a doorbell to the left of the door. I pushed it, but I didn't hear any ringing inside, so I opened the screen door and knocked on the inside one. Rebecca edged backward, like she didn't want to be associated with me anymore. But when no one answered, she said, "Maybe you should knock again."

I didn't have to. The inside door creaked open and a woman looked out at us. Her hair was all messed up and her face was puffy, which made me think we had woken her up.

"Is Amanda here?" I said.

"Around back," the woman said and started to close the door.

"Around back?" I said.

"In the garage," the woman said. The door shut in my face.

I turned and looked at Rebecca.

"Around back," I said.

Rebecca stepped aside to let me go down the porch steps first. She followed me around the side of the house and along the narrow laneway. The whole yard was closed in by a wooden fence that was so high that even if I stood on tiptoe and reached up, I couldn't have touched the top of it. A tired old garage leaned to one side at the back of the yard, like it was getting ready to lie down and go to sleep. The big front door, the one a car would go through, was shut. I went up on my toes and looked through one of the small windows that ran in a row across the top of the door. The window was crusted with grime — Riel would have had me scrubbing it with a sponge and bucket of soapy water if it had been his — but I could make out someone inside, near the back. It was a girl. She was rooting around in a pile of stuff at the back of the garage.

"I think that's her in there," I said to Rebecca in a quiet voice. Rebecca nodded. She wasn't nearly as confident here as she had been in the video store. I led the way around to the side of the garage where there was another door. I thought about knocking, but decided not to. Instead, I pushed the door open and stepped inside.

The girl was on her knees in one of the most clut-
tered garages I had seen in my life. There were
boxes and bags of stuff — it was impossible to tell
what was in most of them — along with broken-
down furniture, a pile of old car tires, a couple of
rusted old rotary lawnmowers and a work table —
homemade, from the look of it — with a bunch of
tools scattered all over it. Riel had a workbench
and lots of tools down in one part of his basement.
But his things were a million times neater than
these.

"Amanda Brown?" I said.

Her head spun around faster than the girl's in
The Exorcist and she had pretty much the same
look on her face.

"Who are you?" she said. "And who said you could
come in here? This is private property."

"Your mother told us you were back here," I said.

She gave me a sour look. "My *mother?*"

I guessed that whoever we had just talked to was
not Amanda Brown's mother.

"The woman in the house," I said.

Amanda Brown stood up slowly. She looked me
over, then she checked out Rebecca. I couldn't tell
whether or not she remembered Rebecca from the
funeral.

"Who *are* you anyway?" she said.

"I'm Mike. This is Rebecca."

Amanda was standing at the back of the garage
with her arms folded over her chest. She looked
pissed off.

"I mean, what do you want?" she said. "What are you doing here?"

"It's about that woman who was killed in that convenience store robbery," I said. "You knew her, right?"

"Says who?"

"You were at the funeral," Rebecca said. "We saw you. I spoke to you."

Amanda's eyes shifted to Rebecca. "Yeah? So?"

"So you wouldn't have gone to the funeral if you didn't know her," Rebecca said.

Amanda shrugged. "A friend of mine lives near there. She goes in the store all the time. I went to the funeral with her. So what?"

"A friend of *mine* was in a store last Friday when it got robbed," I said.

"Yeah?" she said. "And?"

"And he says you were in the store when it happened."

"Excuse me?"

"My friend. He says you were in the store when it was robbed."

When I talk to Rebecca, she always reacts. I'd be lying if I said I always knew what she was thinking, but I could always tell she was thinking something. But this girl? She'd have made a killer gambler. She didn't react at all. There was no expression on her face. She just looked at me and waited. When I didn't say anything — two can wait — she said, "I don't know what your friend is talking about."

"You're saying you weren't in the store?"

"Yeah. That's what I'm saying. Because I wasn't in the store."

I glanced at Rebecca. I still couldn't tell what Amanda was thinking, but I had a pretty good idea about Rebecca. She was thinking that she didn't like Amanda Brown. Maybe she was even thinking Amanda Brown was one of the bitchiest girls she had ever met. For sure she was one of the toughest girls I had ever met. I could picture her and Rebecca going at it.

I stepped between the two of them.

"We know that you were caught shoplifting in the store," I said. I tried to make it sound like it wasn't a big deal.

"Yeah?" Amanda said. "Says who?"

"A man we talked to. He was in the store. He's the one who caught you."

She didn't like that.

"That's his story," she said. "Old fart. He comes in while I'm trying to decide what to buy and he sees what I look like and the next thing I know he's grabbing me by the arm and hauling me up to the cash saying I'm stealing and that he's going to call the cops, that's the only way to handle people like me. What does that even mean — people like me?"

I was willing to bet Rebecca had an answer to that.

"But Mrs. Lee didn't call the police, did she?" I said. "In fact, she helped you get the job at the video store." I was pretty sure I'd get a reaction to that, too — How did we know she worked at a video store? But her face showed nothing. She just looked at me, her arms still crossed over her chest. "That's why you went to the funeral, right? Because she didn't call the cops on you. Because she helped you get a job. She was nice, right?"

"Did *you* know her?" Amanda Brown said.

"No."

"Then how do you know what she was like?"

"I'm just saying if you were stealing from her and she gave you a chance — "

"Look, you don't know me. You don't know anything about me. You're in my garage. I don't want you here. Go away. Simple, huh?"

"But my friend says you were in the store when it happened."

Her eyes narrowed.

"This friend of yours, is he the one they arrested?"

I glanced at Rebecca, then I nodded.

"Well, your friend is lying. I wasn't there."

"He's pretty sure."

She stared at me.

"The way I heard it, there were three guys in the store when it happened. Someone heard gunshots and saw three guys run out of the store and he identified one of them. That's what people are saying. I never heard anything about that guy saying there was anyone else in the store except the people who were shot." I noticed she didn't say their names, not even Mrs Lee's. She just called them the people who were shot. Mrs. Lee hadn't called the cops on her. She had helped her get a job. But Amanda Brown was acting like she didn't care. What did that mean? "So, three bad guys and two people who were shot. That's who I heard was in that store. Which means if your friend was in the store, he's a thief and a killer."

She was pretty if you looked at her a certain way. Her hair was a light blond colour, short, kind of perky. Her skin was pale. She wasn't wearing any jewellery. No eyebrow ring. If she had a tattoo, it was hidden under her sweatshirt. She seemed kind of sweet — if you looked at her in a certain way. But looking at her now, with her hard blue eyes and her sour mouth and the contempt in her voice, there was nothing pretty about her. She came across as nasty and bitter and mean.

"My friend says he didn't do anything. He just happened to be there. He says he saw you in there and that you saw everything that happened and that you could tell the police that he had nothing to do with it."

She nodded, but not because she was agreeing with me.

"So let me get this straight," she said. "You're telling me that you think I was in a store and saw a woman get killed — a woman who, according to you, gave me some kind of break — " Boy, she was backing right off even knowing Mrs. Lee. " — but that I didn't go to the police and tell them what happened and what I supposedly saw so that they could actually go out and nail the guys that did it. Is that what you're telling me?" She shook her head. "I wasn't there. I wasn't in the store. I don't know what your friend is trying to pull, but he's wrong."

I glanced at Rebecca. She looked lost, like she thought she had made her way to the right place only to find out that she had read the map upside down and backward.

"I can go to the cops," I said. "I can tell them you're the one my friend saw."

"Yeah? You mean your friend got arrested, but he didn't tell the cops he saw me there? He just told you?"

I didn't answer.

"Uh-huh," Amanda Brown said. "The cops didn't believe him, huh? What makes you think they're going to believe you — especially since you don't know what you're talking about? You want to go to the cops? Go ahead. I'll tell them the same thing I told you. I wasn't there. I don't know what your friend is trying to pull, but if you ask me, he must be neck-deep in crap if he's seeing things that weren't there."

"He described you perfectly," I said. "He described your tattoo."

"Really?" she said. "That doesn't prove a thing. A lot of people have the same tattoo. Maybe he's confusing me with someone else. Or maybe he's just seen me around someplace."

Nothing fazed her. It was starting to get to me. I

couldn't shake her, and the fact that I couldn't was shaking my confidence in Vin.

"So you're saying you weren't there?" I said.

"Are you deaf as well as stupid? That's exactly what I'm saying."

I stared at her. She stared at me. Someone tugged my arm. Rebecca.

"Come on, Mike. Let's get out of here."

"Yeah, Mike," Amanda Brown said. "Listen to your preppy girlfriend and get out of my garage."

Rebecca grabbed my hand and yanked me out of the garage. She marched down the driveway as fast as she had marched into that first video store. She didn't slow down until we were a couple of blocks from Amanda Brown's house.

"Do you believe her?" I said.

"Do you think I look preppy?" Rebecca said.

It was one of those questions I didn't know how to answer, but that I knew she wanted me to. "You look great," I said. "All the time."

Rebecca stretched out her arms as if she were standing in front of a mirror, checking herself out. Then she looked at me and shook her head.

"You don't even know what preppy looks like, do you, Mike?" she said.

I didn't know how to answer that, either, but this time she didn't expect me to.

She looped an arm through mine and we started to walk up the street.

"I don't know if I believe her or not," she said. "But I sure don't like her."

"Why would Vin say she was there if she wasn't there? How would he be able to describe her so well?"

Rebecca shook her head.

"Why would she say she wasn't there if she was?" she said.

One more of those questions.

"Hey, Rebecca? That Megan, the one who runs the store, you know her, right?"

"Yeah. She's the one who gave me all those coupons."

"You think maybe we could talk to her?"

Rebecca smiled. "I was thinking the same thing," she said.

* * *

I went straight to work without going home first. Riel had already told me that he was taking Susan out to dinner and then they were going to a movie. He'd told me that they would probably be late and not to wait up for them. When I got home after work, there was a note for me on the fridge. Vin's mother had called again. She wanted me to call her.

The first thing I thought was, Something must have happened to Vin. Why else would his mother be calling me? I remembered his phone number — even after all this time — and dialled it. Vin's mother picked up. Right away she thanked me for calling.

"Is Vin okay?" I said.

She said he was fine.

"I'm going to see him tomorrow afternoon, Mike," she said. "I was hoping you could come with me. He wants to see you. He's having a hard time, Mike. Especially after what happened today."

Today?

"What happened, Mrs. Taglia?"

"The man who was shot — I just heard, Mike. He died."

Oh boy.

"I'll understand if you don't want to come," Vin's mother said. "But it really cheered Vin up when you went to see him earlier in the week and when you spoke to him on the phone."

I could tell from the way she was talking that she was fighting back tears. But even if she hadn't been upset, there was no way I could say no to her. She'd been like a second mother to me, especially after my mother had died.

"What time are you going?" I said.

"I could pick you up after I get off work. Is three-thirty okay?"

I told her sure.

After I hung up the phone, I sat on the couch and stared at the blank TV for a long time. The tape I had made for Susan was sitting on top of it. I picked it up and looked at it. I wondered if Jeremy had at least taped something good. I popped it into the VCR and hit Play. Talk about irony. He had taped *CSI*. I watched the whole thing.

CHAPTER TWELVE

The next day was one of those days that there aren't enough of — a weekday during the school year when you don't have to go to school. It was a professional development day. Riel left the house at the regular time. He was headed downtown to some special conference on teaching history. It sounded like a snooze to me. I still couldn't figure out how someone who used to be a cop, which at least was interesting even if I didn't like cops all that much, could get such a charge out of reading history books and sitting all day with a bunch of other history teachers listening to someone talk about teaching history. But I guess it was none of my business.

It was nearly nine o'clock by the time I rolled out of bed. My head felt like it was stuffed with cotton. I hadn't slept much. I kept thinking about Amanda Brown and why she would lie — assuming she was the one who was lying, not Vin. I stumbled down to the kitchen. Susan was sitting at the kitchen table. She had the newspaper open and was reading it while she drank coffee. When she saw me, she started to get up.

"You want me to fix you something for breakfast, Mike?"

I told her no, it was okay, I'd get my own breakfast. Riel had made it clear to me after he proposed to Susan that some things were going to change and other things weren't. The big thing that was going to change: Susan was going to be around a lot more before the wedding, and afterward she was going to move in. "There's going to be a woman in the house, Mike," he said. "Which means things have to be a certain way, you know?" I think mostly he meant not so much farting. Things that weren't going to change: my chores, which included keeping my room clean, doing my share of the vacuuming and tidying in the rest of the house ("I'm not the only person who uses the living room and the dining room, Mike."), and the cooking. In other words, Riel said, I shouldn't expect Susan to jump up and do things for me that I could do myself just because she was a woman. I never would have expected that, but Riel made the point all the same.

I was just getting myself some cereal when the doorbell rang.

Susan looked up from her paper. "I'll get it," I said.

I saw through the glass before I even opened the door that it was Detective Canton and Detective Mancini. I wanted to walk away from the door and leave them both standing out there, but I knew I couldn't. Besides, it would just make them angry. I unlocked the door and opened it.

"Good morning, Mike," Detective Canton said, like it was the best morning of his life so far. "Is Riel around?"

"He's at a conference."

156

"Well, that's okay. You can call him from the police station."

The police station?

"Are you arresting me?" I said. It had to be a joke, but it didn't feel funny.

"We want you to come with us. We want to ask you some questions."

"About what?"

Detective Mancini grinned at me. It was not a pretty sight.

"Bad news, Mike," he said. "Someone dropped a dime on you."

"Huh?" What did that even mean?

"That Crime Stoppers announcement I told you about?" Detective Canton said. "Someone called in. Swears they saw you go into that store just before it was robbed."

"What?"

"So we want you to come with us, Mike. You can call Riel when you get there."

"Is he under arrest?" someone said behind me. Susan.

Both detectives turned their heads to look at her. She was standing in the doorway to the living room.

"And you are?" Detective Canton said.

"Dr. Susan Thomas."

"Doctor?"

"That's right."

"And your relationship to Mike?" Detective Canton said.

"To Mike? None. I'm engaged to John Riel." I don't think I imagined the appreciative look on his face when he looked at Susan — heck, why not? Susan was pretty *and* smart. "Why do you want to talk to Mike?" she said.

Detective Canton told her what he had already told me. She asked him again if I was under arrest. He told her no, not at this time, but that they wanted to question me further.

"Fine," she said. "Let me call John." She dialled the number for his cell, but he didn't answer. "He's at a conference," she said. "He probably turned off his phone." She looked at me. "I'll go with you, Mike." I knew she was doing it to make me feel better, but it didn't work. Someone had called the cops on me. Someone had said that I had gone into the store right before it was robbed. Who would do something like that? No offence to Susan, but I would rather have had Riel with me. He knew how things worked. He also knew how cops worked. Then Susan surprised me. She said, "That is, *if* you want to go, Mike." She looked at Detective Canton. "You said he's not under arrest, right? So you can ask him to go to the police station, but you can't force him to. Right?"

Detective Canton looked at Detective Mancini. Then he nodded.

"That's right."

"I know you told him what you wanted to question him about," Susan said. "But did you tell him what the consequences might be if he goes with you and answers your questions?"

The two detectives exchanged glances again.

"We were going to get to that," Detective Canton said. "We do these things by the book."

"I think you should tell him now," Susan said. She crossed her arms and waited. Detective Mancini looked annoyed. Detective Canton sighed and looked at me.

"If you come and talk to us," he said, "charges may result and any statement you make may later be used in court."

Susan's face got more serious. "Did you explain to him about consent?"

"Given his track record, I think he already knows about consent," Detective Mancini said.

Susan gave him a sour look.

"Mike, you don't have to come in for questioning at this time," Detective Canton said. "The choice is yours. If you do come in, you are free to leave at any time during the questioning — at this point." I knew why he said it like that: because even if he didn't consider me a suspect now, that could change once he was actually talking to me. Then he would have to stop and give me another caution. "We'll go over this again when you get to the police station and make sure you understand what's happening and what your rights are. Then you'll sign a consent form. Do you understand?" I said I did. Finally he looked at Susan. "Okay?"

Susan was frowning.

"I think we should wait until we can get hold of

John," she said. She looked at the two detectives. "I'll get John to call you when he's free. He's Mike's foster parent. He's responsible."

"It's okay," I told Susan. "We can go now." I wanted to get it over with, and who knew how long Riel was going to be at his conference.

"I don't know, Mike," Susan said. "We should at least call a lawyer."

"But I didn't do anything," I said.

She hesitated for a long time before she finally said, "Where do I bring him?"

"We'll take you," Detective Canton said.

"I'd prefer to drive him myself," Susan said.

They told her where to meet them and then they left the house. But they didn't drive away. Instead, they sat in their car out in front of the house while Susan went upstairs to change. While I waited for her, I thought about the videotape that I had made for her. I wished I had mentioned it to the cops the first time they'd asked me about that night. If I told them about it now, they'd probably think I was making it up. They'd be really suspicious about whether it was for real. I dropped it into my backpack anyway, just in case.

Susan came back downstairs, grabbed her keys, and pulled on a jacket. The two cops were still out there when we went outside. They watched us as we walked from the house to the street, where Susan had parked her car. They watched us drive away. Then they followed us. I think that made Susan nervous, which made me nervous. I wondered if I should tell her what I was thinking, but she kept looking in the rearview mirror at the cop car. I started to think she'd been right — we should have waited for Riel.

When we got to the police station Detective Canton read me my rights and made me sign that I understood. Susan listened carefully the whole time. Then Detective Canton asked me to explain how come someone had seen me go into the store just before it was robbed.

"Who saw him?" Susan said.

Detective Canton didn't answer.

"You said it was someone who called Crime Stoppers," Susan said. "Crime Stoppers doesn't ask for names, does it? It doesn't even have call display on its phones. If someone calls in and gives information, they get a special reference number so that if an arrest is made on the basis of that information, they can use that number to get a reward. It's all anonymous, isn't it?"

I stared at her. How did she know all that?

Detective Canton asked me again why someone would say they'd seen me go into the convenience store last Friday night just before the Lees were shot.

"I don't know," I said. "They must be mistaken." Or lying. But who would lie about me like that? "I already told you, I was home that night."

"The person who called didn't just give an accurate description of you, Mike," Detective Canton said. "They gave your name. How do you explain that?"

There was only one answer to that. "They were lying."

"Right," Detective Mancini said. "Your best friend Vincent Taglia is seen running out of the store. We find him with some of the stolen money on him. He claims he doesn't know who the guys were who did it. Claims he can't even describe them. You're with him when he gets arrested. You claim you haven't seen him in months, but you go and visit him while he's in detention. You talk to him on the phone, too. All of a sudden you're in a lot of contact with a guy you claim you haven't had any contact with in months. And your pal Sal gets beaten up as a warning for him not to say anything. But the person who called Crime Stoppers, *that* person is lying. Is that it, Mike?"

"I don't care what you think," I said. "I was home the whole night."

"Home *alone*," Detective Mancini said. "With no one to back you up." He was staring at me as if I were a piece of garbage, which made me even more nervous than I already was. I was afraid that he wouldn't believe anything I said. But I had to try. I focused on Detective Canton, who was slightly less scary than Detective Mancini.

"That store was robbed around ten o'clock last Friday night, right?" I said.

Detective Canton nodded.

"And you said someone called Crime Stoppers and said they saw me go into the store just before then, right?"

Detective Canton nodded again.

I sucked in a big breath. They weren't going to believe me. I knew they weren't. But I had to do something, and maybe Susan could help to convince them. I could feel my face turning red when I told them that I had turned the TV on at around eight, had watched it for a while, and then, at nine-thirty, had turned on the VCR and had sat there for the next hour and a half taping the final episode of Susan's favourite TV program and a special about it. My cheeks burned as I told him which program it was.

"That's the one about those women in Manhattan, right?" Detective Canton said.

"I taped it for Susan," I said. I glanced at her. She had that same I'm-so-sorry-Mike look on her face that she'd had when she told me the bad news about what had happened to the tape. "There's no way I could have been at that store at ten o'clock because I was home taping that program."

Detective Mancini shook his head.

"You could have programmed the VCR to record it while you were out," he said.

That's when Susan interrupted. I guess she decided we had nothing to lose.

"But Mike knows I don't like watching commercials," she said, "so he sat there and stopped the tape whenever a commercial came on and started it again when the commercials were over. I know. I watched the tape."

"You can program a VCR to skip the commercials," Detective Canton said.

"You can program *some* VCRs to do that," Susan said. "But you can't program John's to do it. It's practically first generation. John doesn't believe in throwing away anything that still works."

Boy, did she ever know Riel.

"If you watched the tape, you could see places where Mike was a little slow on the Play button after the commercials ended, or a little slow pressing Pause when the commercials came on," she told the detectives. "If Mike had used a VCR that could skip commercials, you wouldn't see that."

Detective Mancini was still shaking his head.

"He could have asked someone else to tape the program for him," he said. "That way, he could use it as an alibi."

"True," Susan said. "But if that were the case, don't you think when he gave me the tape — the day *after* the robbery — that he would have made a big deal about it? Don't you think if he got that show taped just to have an alibi, he would have told you about it right away? When you first talked to him, did he mention the tape? Did he tell you what he was doing? No, he just said he was watching TV, right?"

Detective Canton had to admit that she was right.

"He didn't mention the tape when he talked to you, and he didn't make a big deal about it when he gave it to me," Susan said. "He just slipped it to me and told me it was a surprise. Does that sound like someone who was establishing an alibi?"

I glanced at the two detectives, but I couldn't tell what they were thinking.

"He didn't say anything about it because he was embarrassed about watching the program, weren't you, Mike?"

I nodded and held my breath. Then Detective Mancini asked the question that I had been dreading.

"I don't suppose you happen to have this videotape, do you?" he said.

Susan sagged in her chair and got that sorry look on her face again.

"I lent the tape to a friend of mine. Her son taped over it," she said.

Detectives Canton and Mancini exchanged glances. Detective Mancini rolled his eyes, like trying to use a videotape that had already been taped over was the lamest thing he had ever heard of.

"I have it in my backpack," I said. Susan gave me a look. I knew what she was thinking: What good would it do? "It's true what Susan told you," I said. "Her friend's son taped over it. He taped an episode of *CSI*."

"Well I guess that makes you flat out of luck," Detective Mancini said. I knew he was probably just playing bad cop to Detective Canton's not-so-bad cop, but he scared me anyway.

"*CSI* is only an hour long," I said, trying to sound more confident than I felt. "The show I taped was ninety minutes."

"So?" Detective Mancini said.

"So if you fast-forward, you can see the last part of the show I taped. You can see what Susan said — where I tried to skip the commercials and where I was a little off." I reached for my backpack.

Susan was almost smiling as she said, "And I'd be happy to give you my friend's name. She'll confirm that that's the tape I gave her. And her son can confirm that that's his handwriting on the label — he put that on the cassette after he taped his program." She took a notepad and pen out of her purse, wrote something on it — her friend's name and phone number, I guess — tore out the page and handed it to Detective Canton, who studied both it and the videocassette.

"Oh," Susan said, "and if you're thinking maybe he taped it at some other time, you'd better check your TV listings. The program was only aired the one time. It was a real event."

She smiled at me. She was amazing. I thought Riel had made a good decision when he proposed to her. I hoped he wasn't going to mess things up.

The two detectives looked at each other.

"I bet you get a lot of tips on Crime Stoppers that don't lead anywhere," Susan said. "I bet there are people out there who even give you false tips, you know, given that callers don't have to identify themselves and aren't asked for a name. This kind of thing must happen from time to time."

Neither detective said anything.

"So, do you have any other questions for Mike?"

"Not at this time, no," Detective Canton said.

"Can I have a receipt for that videotape?" Susan said politely.

We waited while they got Susan what she wanted. She looked at me, but didn't say anything until after we were back in her car. Then, as she pulled out onto the street, she said, "When did you find out about the tape?"

"Just last night. I didn't even have time to tell you about it before Canton and Mancini turned up this morning. Then, on the way to the station, I was trying to figure out what I was going to say to them."

"Well, good thinking, Mike," she said.

"Thanks for coming with me, Susan. You were great," I said. "How did you know what to say to them? Before we left the house, I mean?"

She shrugged. "The police come around Emerg sometimes and want to talk to someone I'm treating. If you have to deal with them, it makes sense to know what they can and can't do. John filled me in. But you handled yourself really well, Mike." She smiled at me for a moment. Then her face got serious again. "You know what I wish, Mike? I wish they had call display at Crime Stoppers, because I wish they could catch whoever called in that so-called tip and charge them with filing a false report. It's probably just a prank. But it's not a funny one, is it?"

She had that right. All the way home, I thought about who could have called the cops on me. Whoever it was knew my name and what I looked like, which meant it was someone I knew — or

167

someone who knew me. But who would do that to me? And why?

* * *

When Susan and I got back to the house, there was a message on the phone: "It's Rebecca. It's eleven o'clock on Friday morning. Can Mike please call me?"

I checked my watch. It was eleven-fifteen. I started to punch in her number, but stopped when Susan said, "Mike?" I put the receiver down. "I have to go," Susan said. She said she had to get to work. She told me she was sure everything was going to be fine now. She told me she'd tried again to get hold of Riel, but hadn't been able to. She said that she'd left a message for him to call her and that when he did, she would explain to him what had happened. She told me not to worry.

After she left, I called Rebecca, who said, "How fast can you get over here?"

"Ten minutes if I run," I said.

"Run, Mike."

"Yeah, but — "

"It's important."

I locked the front door and jogged all the way to Rebecca's house. It took me eight minutes.

The door to her house opened almost as soon as I knocked. Rebecca pulled me inside and dragged me through to the kitchen. A slim woman with brown hair and brown eyes was sitting at the kitchen table, holding a coffee mug.

"Mike, this is Megan Doherty. Megan, this is Mike McGill."

Megan smiled at me. "Becca was just telling me about you," she said.

Becca? I'd never heard her called that before.

"And Megan was telling *me* about Cecilia Lee," Rebecca said. "Sit down, Mike."

I dropped into an empty chair.

"The church Megan goes to works with an agency that helps new Canadians get settled."

"There's a group of us at the church who volunteer with the agency," Megan said. "They pair us up with someone who's new to the country. We meet them for coffee or whatever, answer their questions, help them practise their English, show them around the city."

"Megan was paired with Cecilia Lee," Rebecca said.

Megan nodded.

"When Cecilia first arrived, she barely spoke English. She was from a small village in China. She found it very intimidating living in the middle of a big city. And, of course, she married someone she didn't really know and who was twenty-something years older than her."

"Megan got to know Cecilia well," Rebecca said.

"I don't know if I'd say *well*," Megan said. "We had a language barrier at first. And her husband wasn't exactly thrilled about her going out to have coffee with me. To be honest, I think he would have preferred it if she never left the store. When she started coming to church, he gave her a hard time about that."

"Megan didn't like Mr. Lee," Rebecca said.

"I tried to keep an open mind," Megan said. "But after a while, Cecilia began to cancel our meetings, and it was always because her husband needed her to do this or that. Finally I started going to the store to see her. He didn't like that, either, but I refused to let him chase me off. I felt sorry for her. She told me that she didn't mind working hard or putting in long hours. She thought that would mean she could send money home to her family. She had three younger sisters, and she promised she would send them gifts. But it didn't work out that way. Her husband never gave her a dime. He bought all the food, paid all the bills, bought all of her clothes — not that he exactly went broke on that."

"Didn't you hear?" I said. "He died yesterday."

"Oh," Megan said. The news seemed to shake her. "I'm sorry. What I said — it must have sounded terrible."

"You didn't know," Rebecca said. It looked to me like Rebecca hadn't heard either.

I didn't see what the big deal was. If the guy was a creep when he was alive, how did his dying change anything?

"Why didn't she just leave him?" I said. "I mean, if he treated her that way."

"I think she was afraid to," Megan said. "I got the impression that her family wouldn't have approved if the marriage didn't work out. Then she got pregnant. But this guy, her husband . . . " She shook her head. "She told me that he emptied the cash register regularly — as if he was afraid she'd take money and spend it on something for herself. Cecilia told me that the most money he kept in the register was one hundred dollars, and a lot of that was coins — you know, loonies and toonies. The rest he kept locked in his metal box."

Metal box? Sal had said something about a box. So had Vin.

"You mean, like a lock box?" I said.

Megan nodded.

"Tell Mike about Amanda," Rebecca said.

Megan sighed. "According to Cecilia, the first time Amanda came into the store, another customer accused her of shoplifting. That customer wanted Cecilia to call the police. But Cecilia isn't like that. She's the kind of person who always tries to understand other people. You know, who always gives someone a second chance."

"So she let Amanda go," I said.

Megan nodded. "I wouldn't have. But who knows? Maybe Cecilia knew what she was doing."

"Why do you say that?"

"Because Amanda came back the next day and apologized. At least, that's what Cecilia told me. I thought she must have misunderstood, but she insisted. She said Amanda apologized and even offered to pay for what she'd taken. She said Amanda stayed around for a while and talked to her. I never really figured out how, but the two of them seemed to hit it off. Cecilia's husband didn't

171

approve, of course. Especially of Amanda — I mean, just the way she dressed. Cecilia told me he came in one time when Amanda was there, took one look at her and chased her out. Apparently the man who caught Amanda stealing had described her to Cecilia's husband. He told Cecilia she was never to allow Amanda into the store. Cecilia told me all he saw was her hair and her tattoo. That's what he called her, The Tattoo. That bothered Cecilia."

"I bet Mr. Lee didn't scare Amanda," I said.

Megan shook her head. "Amanda started going to the store when Cecilia's husband was away. I dropped by one time when she was there. She and Cecilia were talking and looking at fashion magazines. Cecilia was laughing. She looked really happy. And her English was improving fast — she was learning all the designers' names. She asked me about some stores downtown that Amanda had told her about and how expensive they were. She said she wished she could buy things like that for her sisters — you know, really nice things, expensive things instead of just the basics." Megan shook her head again. "Then, when I got a new job as manager of a video store, Cecilia asked me to help Amanda by giving her a job, even though she had no experience and no references. I took her on part-time, fifteen hours a week, as a favour to Cecilia."

"We heard you fired her pretty soon after you hired her," Rebecca said.

"She lasted two weeks. She was late all the time.

I tried to be understanding — I know she doesn't have the best home life."

"What do you mean?"

"Her mother died when she was a child. Her father has had a bunch of girlfriends. And, according to Cecilia, the father drinks a lot. I gather life around Amanda's house is pretty miserable, and I'm sorry about that. But what could I do? The rest of the staff was complaining. It wasn't fair to them that Amanda showed up late all the time. I knew I was going to have to let her go. Then she left me with no choice." She hesitated. "I caught her stealing. DVDs mostly. I didn't want to press charges. It can be such a hassle, all that court time. And I didn't want the district office to know I'd used such poor judgment — we're supposed to insist on references and we're supposed to check them before we hire anyone. It was bad enough that I hadn't done that. But to have that person turn out to be a thief? I didn't want the grief. So I put down the loss as shoplifting and put in Amanda's record that she was let go because she was habitually late." She looked at Rebecca. "I'm glad in a way that I didn't get the chance to tell Cecilia what happened. She would have been so disappointed. For some reason, Cecilia believed in her. Me — to be honest, I started to wonder if Amanda was hanging around Cecilia's store because she wanted to steal from there, too. I feel terrible that I couldn't make it to her funeral. I had a meeting at head office that I couldn't get out of."

I kept thinking about the lock box.

"Where did Mr. Lee keep that metal box?" I said.

"I have no idea," Megan said. "I saw him with it up at the cash that one time. He and Cecilia lived in an apartment above the store. Maybe he kept it there. He also had a sort of office in the storeroom at the back of the store. He could have kept it there." She shrugged. "I don't know. I didn't ask. I didn't think it was any of my business."

After that, Rebecca and Megan talked some more, mostly about Rebecca's sister and a bunch of other people I didn't know. I listened for a while, and then I told Rebecca I had to leave. She walked me to the door. When I filled her in on what had happened with the cops, she hugged me.

"I knew it was going to be okay," she said.

I didn't tell her that I hadn't been nearly so confident or that I still wasn't one hundred percent convinced they believed me.

"I'm going downtown this afternoon, Mike," Rebecca said. "You want to come?"

"I can't," I said. "I have some stuff I have to do."

"I'm going dress shopping," she said.

Boy, one more reason not to go with her.

"I'm going dress shopping," she said, "because of the dance that's happening at school in a couple of weeks."

What? "Did someone invite you to the dance?" I said.

"Not yet, Mike. But that's okay. I'm going to invite him."

Wait a minute! She was going to invite someone to a dance at *our* school?

"You want to go to the dance with me, Mike?" She flashed me a smile.

"I'm sorry, Rebecca," I said.

"Is that a no?"

"I mean, I should have asked you, right?"

"It doesn't matter who asks. Just so long as you want to go with me. You do, don't you?"

I said of course I did. I'd never been to a dance before. I didn't even know how to dance. But if Rebecca wanted to go, well, maybe she'd be happy with just the slow dances.

"Great," she said. She kissed me on the cheek. "I'll be back around five. You want to do something later?"

I said sure. Half the time I couldn't believe she wanted to spend as much time with me as she did.

"Call me," she said. "Promise?"

Like she had to ask.

CHAPTER THIRTEEN

I recognized the Taglias' car when it pulled up outside Riel's house. Vin's mother got out. She looked tired, but she smiled when she saw me.

"Mike," she said, "I almost didn't recognize you. You've grown so much."

I used to be shorter than Vin. Now I was taller. Other than that, though, I didn't think I'd changed much.

I got into the car and we drove the first few minutes in silence. Then Vin's mother said, "We've missed you, Mike. Both Joe and I have." She meant Vin's father. "How are things working out with John Riel? You like living with him?"

I told her I did. "He's kind of strict," I said. "But he's fair."

"I was sorry how things turned out between you and Vin," she said. "You two used to be such close friends. I can't help thinking that if he'd stuck with you instead of hanging around with those other kids, he wouldn't have got himself into so much trouble."

The other kids she meant were Cat Phillips and A.J. Siropoulos. Vin had started hanging around with them after I moved in with Riel. Riel didn't let me go out until I'd done all my homework. He insisted I hold down a part-time job. It didn't leave a whole lot of extra time, so Vin had moved on.

"I'm worried about him, Mike. We both are. He

says he didn't have anything to do with that convenience store robbery, but the police don't believe him and I guess after what happened last fall, I can't really blame them. But he swore to me he wasn't involved." She glanced at me. "And he's having a hard time in there. I thought maybe it would be a little easier this time. I know it sounds terrible, but I thought maybe he'd be used to it. But I can tell he's scared and worried. I'm glad you went to see him — I think it really made him feel better. And I'm glad you're coming with me now."

She talked like she was nervous, like if she didn't keep talking, we would both feel awkward. And I realized that although I used to see her a lot — because Vin and Sal and I used to hang out at Vin's place — I had never spent any time alone with her. And now that I was alone with her, I didn't know what to say. Maybe she felt the same way. So I let her talk about Vin and when she was finished, I told her a little more about school and Riel and my job at the community centre. I was glad when we finally arrived at the detention centre.

We went through the sign-in and then security, and then they let us go into the visiting room where we waited for Vin.

He looked even worse than the last time I had seen him. He was pale and he looked thinner and tired. But he smiled when he saw his mother and he hugged her and then he said, "Hey, Mike, thanks for coming."

We all sat down at a table, Vin on one side, Vin's

mother and I on the other. Vin's mother asked him how the food was and whether he was sleeping okay, and Vin said it was fine and, yeah, he was sleeping, even though you could see that it wasn't true. She said that his father would have come, but he was doing some overtime at the Ford plant where he worked and how that would come in handy to pay the lawyer. Vin sort of winced when he heard that. Whatever he'd done or hadn't done, I could see he felt bad that his mother had to pay a lawyer because of it and maybe had to give up some things to make sure that the legal bills got paid. Then I remembered how, no matter what, Vin had always managed to scrape together some money somehow to get his mother something nice on her birthday and again for Christmas. Finally he said, "Mom, I'd like to talk to Mike alone for a few minutes, okay?"

She nodded.

"I'll be outside," she said.

Vin waited until she left the room. Then he said, "You can't believe what it's like in here, Mike. I hope you never find out."

"I had to go down to the police station again this morning, Vin."

"You're kidding," Vin said. "What for?"

"Someone called them and said they saw me go into the store before it was robbed."

Vin laughed.

"It's not funny, Vin."

"Yeah, it is, Mike, if you look at it the right way. I told them who *was* there — that girl — and they don't believe me. I bet if I tell them who *wasn't* there — you — they wouldn't believe me either. Nice, huh? My life is so messed up, when I tell the truth, everyone thinks I'm lying."

"What did you want to see me about, Vin?"

Vin's face turned serious.

"The man from the store died."

"I know."

"The cops came to see me again. They asked me again about the two guys who were in the store. They said it's two murders now and if I don't tell them who the other two guys were, I'm going to face it all on my own."

He was trying not to show it, but I could see he was scared.

"Did you find the girl?"

I didn't know what to tell him. I didn't want to get his hopes up — *Yeah, I found her* — only to have to disappoint him — *but she swears she wasn't there.* So I said, "Are you sure about the girl, Vin? You wouldn't lie to me about her being there, would you?"

"Lie to you? Are you kidding, Mike? Why would I lie to you about a thing like that? The girl is my ticket out of here." He looked at me. "You haven't had any luck, huh?"

He looked small sitting there in that chair, thinking about all the trouble he was in. I thought maybe I should tell him what Rebecca and I had found out so that at least he would know that I'd tried. But if I did, he'd want to tell the cops or his lawyer or someone. And if the cops checked it out, if they went to Amanda, she'd do exactly what she said she would — she'd swear she wasn't there. She'd say she didn't know what they were talking about. And the cops, who already didn't believe Vin, would probably believe her. After all, no one else had seen a girl in the store. And that would be that. Telling him now wouldn't do any good. Worse, it would confirm to the police that he was lying — as if they needed more confirmation. But maybe if I tried one more time . . .

"We thought we had a lead, but it didn't pan out," I said.

"We?"

"Me and Rebecca."

"Rebecca?"

I kept forgetting how long it had been since we'd talked regularly and what he knew and didn't know.

"You know, the girl who was walking by the park that night."

His eyes widened in surprise.

"Rebecca with the red hair?"

I nodded.

"You're going out with her, Mikey?"

"Yeah. She's nice."

"Well, she's pretty."

"Pretty and smart," I said. "She's been helping me look for the girl. But so far we haven't had much luck." I felt terrible lying to him. "I'm going to keep trying, though."

"Thanks, Mike," he said. He looked tired and sad and disappointed.

Now there was something I had to ask him. "Vin, those guys who robbed the store. Did you see them take the money from the woman?"

Vin nodded. "Yeah," he said. "But from behind. I saw the woman hand over some cash, but I didn't see the guys."

"Did she give them anything else?"

"What do you mean? Like what?"

"Like a lock box. You know, a metal box with a key. Locked."

He perked up. "The cops asked me about a box. They asked me where it was. But I didn't know what they were talking about. A lock box, huh? What was in it? Money?"

"The old man emptied the cash register regularly. He kept most of his money in a lock box. Did Mrs. Lee give those two guys the box?"

"If she did, I didn't see it."

"Did you see the guys leave the store?"

"Yeah. After they shot the man, they split. Fast."

"Did you see if they were carrying a box?"

"This lock box, you mean?"

"Yeah."

He stared off into space for a minute, like he was trying to picture it. Then he shook his head.

"I don't think they were carrying anything. I saw them run. I'm pretty sure I would have noticed if they were carrying a box. Why? Did the cops say something to you about it?"

I shook my head. "I just remember you saying the police asked you about it," I said. "That's all." But that wasn't all. I was wondering about that box and remembering what Sal had said — the old man had asked him where the box was. The police had asked Vin the same question. That meant the box was missing. If the guys who'd robbed the store hadn't taken it, who had?

I went and got Vin's mother and I waited outside while she visited a little longer with Vin. Then she drove me home.

* * *

No one was home when I got there, but there was a message on the phone from Rebecca — she was setting the record for messages today. This one said: "This is Rebecca for Mike. Mike, call me on my cell as soon as you get this."

I punched in her cell number. She answered on the first ring.

"Where have you been?" she said. "I've been waiting for you to call."

"I'm sorry," I said. "I had to go out. Did you get a nice dress?"

"I saw her, Mike. I saw her, and she was doing some serious shopping. She had bags from half a dozen different stores. Expensive stores."

She? "Who are you talking about, Rebecca?"

"Amanda."

Oh. I had a feeling I was going to regret this, but: "So?"

"You saw where she lived, right, Mike?"

"Yeah."

"And she only worked at that video store for, what, less than two weeks? Fifteen hours a week, and she was late all the time? Isn't that what Megan said?"

"Yeah."

"And she had no work experience, right? Megan said that, too, didn't she?"

"Yeah . . . "

"So that means she wasn't earning money from anywhere else, right?"

"Yeah, I guess."

"So, Mike, I saw her with bags from a bunch of different stores. One of them was from a shoe store where the shoes go minimum a hundred dollars a pair. And they weren't on sale. I checked. Nothing in the store was on sale. And that was just one bag, Mike. The other bags were also from nice stores. I don't mean Wal-Mart. I mean *really* expensive places. Where did someone like Amanda Brown get the money to shop in places like that?"

"What are you thinking, Rebecca?"

"Don't you get it, Mike? Vin says she was in the store. She says she wasn't. Why would she lie? Because she took money from the store, that's why. She was out today spending *stolen* money." I had to hold the receiver away from my ear a little because she was practically yelling the words at me. "We should call the cops, right?"

I hated to ask my next question, but I did. "And tell them what?"

"What do you mean? Tell them what I just told you."

"You mean, tell them that Amanda Brown went shopping?" I said.

"With stolen money."

"*Maybe* with stolen money," I said.

"You said there was blood on the money Vin had when he was arrested. Mike, I remember some of the store bags she was carrying. We can call the cops and tell them what we saw and they can go to the stores and check the money in their registers." There was a pause. "Well, assuming they haven't given any of the money to other customers — you know, as change."

I was shaking my head as I listened to her. "There was blood on the money that Vin had because Cecilia Lee was holding it when she was shot. The money she gave those guys came from the cash register. But if Amanda was spending as much money as you say, Rebecca, it couldn't have come from the cash register. Remember what Megan said? The old guy always emptied the register. He never kept more than a hundred dollars in there. The rest he took out and kept in his lock box."

Wait a minute.

The lock box.

Megan had said she wasn't sure where Mr. Lee kept the box. But she did say that he had a desk in the storeroom in the back. Maybe he kept it there.

Vin was pretty sure that the guys who shot the Lees hadn't taken a box with them.

Vin had said he'd seen Amanda Brown in the storeroom at the back of the store.

Maybe Amanda Brown had taken the box. She'd tried to steal from the store before. She'd stolen DVDs from the video store where she worked. Amanda Brown liked to take things that didn't belong to her. That would explain why she hadn't gone to the police about what she had seen in the convenience store.

She had dyed her hair right after the shooting. She had removed the ring from her eyebrow. Why? Maybe because she didn't want to be recognized. And maybe because up until yesterday, Mr. Lee had still been alive and there was a chance he might recover. Mr. Lee had said something to Sal about a box. Had he been worried that the robbers had taken his lock box? Or had he actually seen someone take it? Had he seen Amanda?

My mind was racing.

Mr. Lee had been able to identify Vin from a picture the police showed him, but he obviously hadn't told the police who took the box. So maybe he hadn't seen Amanda. Or maybe he'd seen her but he'd been too badly hurt to tell anyone. If he had told the police about her, they would have believed Vin when he said there was a girl in the store. But the police didn't believe Vin. So that must mean that Mr. Lee hadn't said anything.

From what I had heard, Mr. Lee cared more about his money than he did about anything else. If he had recovered, he probably would have pestered the police about the lock box. He would have told them where he kept it. If he'd seen who took it or if he'd seen anyone in the storeroom, he would have told them that, too. Even if he hadn't seen Amanda, he might have told them about the girl with the tattoo who had stolen from his store once before. He would have described her — spiky black hair, an eyebrow ring . . . Just like Vin had said.

Except that Amanda didn't have spiky black hair anymore. She didn't have an eyebrow ring, either. Why was that?

Maybe because Amanda Brown had been lying low in case Mr. Lee recovered.

But Mr. Lee hadn't recovered. He was dead. And now Amanda Brown had gone shopping.

"Rebecca, what do you think Amanda Brown was doing in her garage when we found her?" I said.

"What do you mean?"

If Mr. Lee had been serious about keeping his cash safe, the lock box he put it in was probably a sturdy one. And he probably didn't leave the key lying around. For sure he wouldn't leave it wherever he kept the box — what would be the point of that if a thief could take the box and scoop up the key? No, he probably kept the key somewhere safe. If Megan was right about how stingy he was with his wife, he probably kept it someplace where he'd be sure his wife couldn't get at it either. He probably kept it on him.

"Mike?" Rebecca said. "Are you still there?"

"I'm here. Where are you, Rebecca?"

CHAPTER FOURTEEN

I met Rebecca at a coffee shop halfway between downtown and her place. She was drinking coffee but, if you ask me, by the time I got there she was wired enough without the caffeine. I ordered a hot chocolate and sat down across from her.

"Do you think Amanda stole the lock box, Mike?" she said. "Do you think that's why she didn't go to the police and that's why she told us she wasn't there?"

"It sure crossed my mind," I said. I explained what I'd been thinking. Her head bobbed up and down as I talked.

"So we should call the cops and tell them she was in the store, right?"

"We can't say that for sure. We didn't see her. We weren't there."

"Yeah, but if we tell them, they'll go and talk to her."

"And she'll lie to them."

"But Vin already told them — "

"They don't believe him." But the way Amanda lied, I bet they'd believe her. "You know what she's like, Rebecca. She's probably already come up with some convincing story about where Vin might have seen her before. She could say that's how he could describe her." I stared down into my hot chocolate for a moment. "When we saw her, she was rummaging around in that dump of a garage." She'd

187

been pawing through the tools. "How do you open one of those lock boxes, anyway? If you don't have the key, I mean." Then I had another thought. "That garage was a real mess. Did you notice? I bet you could lose a lock box in there," I said. "On purpose, I mean."

Rebecca's eyes glowed. "So you *do* think she took it, don't you, Mike? Do you think she still has it?"

"If she took it," I said slowly, "then I'm pretty sure she still had it yesterday. I bet that was what she was doing in the garage — trying to figure out how to open it."

"Yeah," Rebecca said. "I mean, if you're right, now that Mr. Lee is dead, there's no way the cops are going to be looking for Amanda. And they think the guys who robbed the store took the lock box. You saw that garage, Mike. All she has to do is stash it in a corner of that dump and no one will ever find it. No one will even look."

She was right.

"Unless we call the cops — " she said. She must have read the look on my face, because right away she changed it to, "We can call Crime Stoppers, so it's anonymous. We can tell them Amanda has the lock box from the store. Then *they'll* tell the police and the police will go and search the garage and . . . "

I shook my head.

"It doesn't work that way, Rebecca."

"Sure it does," she said. "The cops get tips all the time. We say we saw her leave the store with the box — "

"But we didn't."

"We don't have to tell them that. We can get creative."

I shook my head again. There was no way I was going to lie to the cops ever again.

"Even if we *got creative*," I said, "the cops wouldn't go and search her garage just on the basis of a tip like that. They can't. They'd have to get a search warrant first. And to get a search warrant, Riel says you have to have probable cause — which they don't have just based on an anonymous tip. They'd have to check her out first. They might even go and talk to her, ask her where she was that night, whether she knew the Lees, stuff like that. And she'll do exactly what she said she'd do — she'll lie to them. They won't be able to arrest her. They won't even be able to search her place right away. And say she does have the box. Say she hasn't got rid of it yet. What's the first thing she's going to do after the cops leave?"

"Get rid of it," Rebecca said. She looked like a kid who had just opened a fancy-wrapped present only to find out it was a box of socks. Then she perked up. "So, why don't we help the cops a little? We can tell them that she's stolen stuff before. If they check her out, they'll find out that she stole from the Lees before *and* from the video store."

"Nobody filed charges against her for those things, Rebecca."

"Yeah, but they could ask Megan."

"You're going to give the cops an anonymous tip

189

and you're going to mention Megan by name?"

"We could just tell them which store it was," Rebecca said.

"That still doesn't make it anonymous," I said. "And it could get Megan in trouble because she didn't give her boss the real reason for firing Amanda. Everyone thinks Amanda got canned because she was late all the time."

"Okay," Rebecca said, deflated. "So we don't mention Megan. We tell them about the old man instead. He's the one who caught her shoplifting."

"*He* says she was shoplifting. *She* says she was going to pay for what she bought and that Mrs. Lee believed her. And since Mrs. Lee didn't file charges . . . "

"Yeah, but if we say we *saw* her with the missing lock box — "

"But we *didn't*."

Rebecca was starting to get exasperated.

"Okay, how about this? Forget the anonymous tip. Forget saying it's a lock box. We just go to the cops and we tell them we saw Amanda Brown leave the store with a box the night of the shooting. Just a box. Let *them* figure out that it's the lock box. We just tell them we think it was a metal box."

I knew she was trying to help, so I hated to have to keep punching holes in her plans. "I already told the cops I was home alone when it happened. If I tell them something different, they'll get suspicious of me all over again."

"Okay, so *I'll* tell them."

"Do you know how much trouble you can get into lying to the police?" I said. *I* sure did. "Especially if you try to say that someone was involved in a crime when they didn't have anything to do with it?"

"She stole the box."

"We think she stole the box."

"I thought we were sure."

"What if we're wrong, Rebecca? What if she was just there, that's all? I'm just saying, before I call the cops or go to the cops and give them a tip, I'd like to be pretty sure that she did something." Especially after what had happened to me this morning. I was pretty sure Amanda Brown was lying about being in the store. And I didn't like her. She was one of those hard girls. But did I want her to have to go through what I'd gone through without being one hundred percent positive she'd done something illegal?

"Boy, Mike, I thought this was going to be easy," Rebecca said. "It actually sounded easy until you started in with probable cause and how cops work."

"Yeah, well, whenever I watch a cop show on TV, Riel always grouses about what they're doing wrong. It really bugs him."

"That's what you get when you live with an ex-cop, I guess," she said. She gave me a funny look. "Mike, do you think Amanda Brown knows as much about probable cause as you do?"

* * *

Rebecca had a plan that wasn't half bad. We used her cell phone to call Amanda, but I made the call because I was the one who had done most of the talking yesterday in her garage. I told her:

"I'm going to give you until tomorrow morning to decide to do the right thing. If you don't go to the cops and tell them the truth about where you were last Friday night when the Lees were shot, I will."

Amanda said, "Good luck."

I told her, "I'm not just going to tell them you were there, which I know you were, Amanda. I'm also going to tell them about the lock box you stole." I'm pretty sure I didn't imagine the little gasp at the other end of the phone. "And I'm going to tell them about the time you were caught shoplifting at the Lees' store and the real reason you got fired from your job at the video store. And then you know what they're going to do, Amanda?" She didn't answer. I hadn't expected her to. "They're going to get a search warrant and they're going to look for that box. And when they find it, you're going to be in a lot more trouble than you would be if you just went and told them that you were there and what you saw."

Amanda said, "Good luck with that, too, Mike." Then she hung up.

"Well?" Rebecca said.

"Well, she's smart enough that she didn't say anything," I said. That was the thing. "She didn't ask me what lock box. She didn't deny it. She didn't say anything a normal person would say." Rebecca gave me a look. "Okay, so she isn't exactly normal. But she didn't say anything except, Good luck."

That's what clinched it for me. "She took that box, Rebecca."

"You think she still has it?"

I sure hoped so, because now I really wanted to get Amanda Brown.

* * *

Fifteen minutes later we were on the corner of the street where Amanda lived. It was just a regular corner, but there was a bus stop on it, which gave us a reason to be standing there. From the bus stop, we could see the front of her house.

"What if she goes out the back?" Rebecca said.

"I guess she could," I said. "But the fence around her yard is pretty high. I don't see her climbing it. Besides, her yard backs right up against another yard, so she'd have to go through that. Maybe her neighbours would make a big stink if she did. Or maybe the neighbours have a dog." The truth was, I didn't know which way she might go. I didn't know if she'd leave the house at all.

By seven o'clock, nothing had happened. I asked Rebecca if I could borrow her phone to call home. There was no answer, which surprised me. I figured Riel would have been back from his conference by then. I left a message to tell him I was out with Rebecca and not to worry about supper, we'd get something to eat.

By eight o'clock the sun had started to go down and I was getting antsy. A lot of buses had passed us and we were still standing at the bus stop. If anyone in the houses nearby had noticed us, they might start wondering why we were hanging around. Some adults don't like kids loitering outside their house. It makes them want to call the cops.

By nine o'clock I was hungry. I'd had breakfast, and I had made myself a peanut butter sandwich before Vin's mother picked me up. But that was it. I started thinking about a nice juicy burger and, yeah, I'd like fries with that.

Then Rebecca said, "Is that her?"

Someone came around the side of Amanda Brown's house — someone small and thin with short blond hair.

"That's her."

She was carrying a shopping bag from a clothing store or a shoe store, the kind that has plastic handles attached to it. She walked down the driveway to the sidewalk and then headed down the street away from us.

"Come on," I said to Rebecca.

We hurried after her. We didn't want to run because she might hear us coming. We were both wearing sneakers and by booting along at double-time we were able to close in on her before she noticed us. I grabbed the bag out of her hand and gave it to Rebecca before Amanda had a chance to react. When Amanda tried to get to Rebecca to get the bag back, I blocked her and held onto her in case she decided to run. Rebecca looked into the bag. Then she looked at me and smiled.

"And I bet it has her fingerprints all over it," Rebecca said.

Amanda stopped squirming.

"Why are you doing this?" she said. "What do you want?"

"I told you. I want you to go to the cops and tell them exactly where you were and what you saw on Friday night. I want you to help clear my friend."

Amanda shook her head. "You're making a big mistake," she said.

CHAPTER FIFTEEN

We went to a hole-in-the-wall restaurant not far
from where Amanda lived, grabbed a booth near
the back, and ordered Coke for me and Amanda
and coffee for Rebecca. I sat on the outside of the
bench next to Amanda so she couldn't take off.
Rebecca sat opposite us and put the bag where
Amanda couldn't reach it.

"It's not what you think," Amanda said.

"Right," Rebecca said. "You didn't steal this box
from the Lees. And you weren't trying to ditch it
before Mike called the cops."

"I took it," Amanda said. "But it wasn't like I
planned it."

"Right," Rebecca said again.

Amanda gave her a dirty look. "Your preppy girlfriend is really annoying, you know that?" she said
to me.

I glanced at Rebecca. She had the bad cop role all
staked out. That left me to be good cop.

"Why *did* you take it?" I said.

"I liked Cecilia Lee," Amanda said. "I know you
probably don't believe it. But I did. She was nice to
me. When that old guy tried to get her to call the
cops on me, she refused. She made him go away.
She told him not to worry. She was always saying
that. No worry, no worry. Then she gave me back
the gum the old guy took off me. That's all it was.
Just a pack of gum."

"Which you were planning to pay for, I suppose," Rebecca said, her tone making it clear she believed *that* the same way she believed in UFOs.

"Cecilia believed me when I said I was. Most people take one look at me — at the way I used to look — and they make assumptions. But not Cecilia. She was nice to me." She was looking right at me now and ignoring Rebecca. Maybe she was lying, but she sure sounded convincing. "So, yeah, I went back the next day to pay for the gum."

Rebecca rolled her eyes. I pressed the toe of my sneaker down on her foot, but gently.

"Believe what you want," Amanda said. "But it's true. I tried to give her the money, but she wouldn't take it. Then her husband came in, and he saw me, and he started screaming at me. I guess the old guy who had caught me must have told him about me. He must have described me. Anyway, her husband started pushing me out of the store and Cecilia tried to stop him. And you know what he did, the creep?"

She looked at me and waited for me to shake my head before she answered.

"He hit her. Right across the face. She almost fell over, he hit her so hard. Then he shoved me out of the place." She glowered across the table at Rebecca. "I bet you didn't read anything like that about him in the paper," she said. "Or see anything like that on the news. It was all, *Poor man, his wife was shot, he was shot, he died. Boo-hoo.* The guy was a creep. He paid for her to come over here and then he held that over her head. He kept telling her, You owe me, you owe me, I paid good money for you. I actually heard him say that one time. She worked long hours in that crummy store. She did all the cooking and cleaning on top of that. And she was pregnant." She shuddered. "That guy was old enough to be her father."

"We know someone who knew Cecilia," Rebecca said. "She didn't say anything about Mr. Lee hitting her."

"You mean Megan from the video store," Amanda said. "She probably didn't know. Cecilia would never have told her. Cecilia would never have told anyone. She was ashamed. She wouldn't even tell her parents when she wrote to them. Or her sisters. She had three sisters back home. She talked about them all the time. They wrote to her regularly. They wanted her to send them stuff — nice stuff."

I thought about all the shopping bags Rebecca had seen Amanda carrying and remembered what Megan had said.

"I only knew what he was like because I saw him do it that time. The next time I went back to the store, I waited until I saw him leave. Then I went in and told her she should call the police on him." She looked at me. "My — my father used to hit my mother all the time. Once they start, they don't stop unless the cops make them." She didn't say anything else for a few seconds. Then, "But Cecilia was afraid to do anything about it. I guess the cops don't have the great reputation back in China that they have here," she said with a sneer.

I looked at Rebecca again. She didn't say anything.

"Anyway," Amanda said, "I started to go by there when her husband was out of the store. He'd go and hang out with a bunch of other old guys at some social club twice a week. He'd leave her alone in the store. And he'd be sure to count the money before he left and when he came back."

I couldn't picture tattoo-eyebrow-ring-spiky-hair Amanda with sweet (according to everyone who had known her) Cecilia Lee.

"What did you two talk about?" I said.

Amanda glared at me. "You mean, what did a punky-looking girl like me have in common with someone like her?" she said. "People like you just see stereotypes. Me — punk. Her — immigrant who didn't speak great English. You didn't know her. She was cool. She liked my hair. And she wanted to know everything. She was always asking me about what people were like here, what they did, why they did it. She never judged anyone."

I was beginning to think that there was more to Amanda Brown that I had imagined.

"I was teaching her more English," she said. "I thought maybe if she could communicate better, she'd be more confident, you know? She'd see she could do better than spend the rest of her life with that old creep."

"What about last Friday night?" I said.

She hesitated.

I nodded toward the bag.

"Rebecca can be out the door and on her way to the cops with that before you can get past me," I said.

She scowled at me, but she said, "Okay, so I was there. Mr. Lee went out to play cards with his old geezer friends, and I went over to keep Cecilia company. I went in the back way. Whenever her husband went out, she opened the back door for me so that I could come in without being seen by any of the nosy neighbours — like that old fart who grabbed me for that pack of gum. He had nothing better to do than watch the neighbours and report to them what was going on. So, yeah, I was there. We were hanging out. Then Cecilia saw her husband pull up in front of the store and she told me to go, get out of there fast. I ran into the storeroom at the back. Mr. Lee came in and told her he'd forgotten something and he was going upstairs to get it. I figured I'd wait in the storeroom until he left. Once he headed back out, he'd be out all night."

I glanced at Rebecca. I don't know what she was thinking, but I had the feeling that this time Amanda was telling the truth. Her face got twisted when she talked about Mr. Lee, but whenever she mentioned Cecilia Lee, it changed. It got a little softer. She really seemed to like her.

"Anyway, I was back there and I heard the bell above the door and this guy came in. Maybe a little shorter than you. Dark hair. Jean jacket or a sweatshirt with a hood, but the hood wasn't up. Jeans.

He walked back to the coolers along the wall where they keep the pop."

"Vin," I said. "That's my friend Vin."

"Whatever," Amanda said.

"He came in alone, right?"

"Yeah. And then maybe, I don't know, ten seconds later, two other guys came in."

"You saw them?"

"Yeah, I saw them."

"Could you describe them?"

She looked at the tabletop.

"Could you describe them?" I said again.

"They were wearing sweatshirts with the hoods up, but there's one of those mirrors above the cash, you know, the kind that's bent so you can see practically the whole store in it. I saw their faces in that, so, yeah, I guess I could describe them."

I glanced at Rebecca. I'm sure she was thinking the same thing I was: if Cecilia Lee was her friend and if she saw who killed her, why hadn't she told the cops?

"Then what happened?" I said.

She sucked in a deep breath. "All of a sudden, one of the guys pulled out a gun and started asking for money. He seemed really jumpy, you know? I thought maybe he was on something. Anyway, he was waving the gun and demanding money while his buddy kept watch out the front window. Cecilia gave him the money that was in the register. Then, *boom,* just like that, he shot her. The next thing I knew, Mr. Lee came through the side entrance into the store — there's an entrance into the store from the apartment upstairs. If you come in that way, you're halfway between the front and back of the store. From there he had a good view of the front of the store, so I knew he saw Cecilia lying on the ground there. They shot her pretty close up, so I can only imagine what she looked like. I saw Mr. Lee turn his head and look in her direction, and then the guy with the gun shot him, too. Then the two of them ran out of the store. A few seconds later, the first guy, your friend, pulled himself together and he ran out after them. He knocked over a bunch of stuff on the way out."

"Pulled himself together?" I said.

"Yeah," Amanda said. "From where I was standing in the storeroom, I could see him pretty good. I saw the look on his face when the jumpy guy pulled the gun. He was *really* surprised. He was like me, I think. He was in shock."

So Vin *hadn't* been in on it. Sal was wrong. Vin wasn't a liar or a killer.

"I was still standing back there. I mean, I couldn't believe it. You ever seen someone get shot? I was shaking all over. And then this other guy came in and he saw Cecilia and then he saw Mr. Lee. He went over to Mr. Lee and do you know what I heard Mr. Lee say to him? He said, 'Did they take my box?' Picture it," Amanda said, her voice shaking with anger. "Say you come into a place and you see Preppy lying on the floor. You can see she's shot and then you get shot, but you're not dead, you can still say something when someone comes in. What's the first thing you'd say? You'd ask about *her,* right? But not Mr. Lee. It was like he didn't care about her at all. All he cared about was his box of money. So as soon as that guy went outside — I think he went to call the cops — I grabbed Mr. Lee's box and I went out the back way. Nobody saw me."

"Were you going to give it back?" Rebecca said.

"When I took it, I didn't know what I was going to do with it. I just wanted to get back at him, you know? So I took it and I ran. Later, after I calmed down, I thought maybe I should call the cops. But then I thought, what if Mr. Lee saw me? What if he thought I had something to do with what happened? He would, you know. He'd tell the cops *I* was involved. And with the trouble I've been in, they'd never believe me if I told them why I took that box. They'd never believe anything I said."

I knew what that was like.

"Even if Mr. Lee didn't see me, he'd make trouble for me if I returned the box," she said.

"You could have dropped it off anonymously," Rebecca said.

Good point.

Amanda glowered at her.

"Yeah," she said. "I could have. But I started thinking about Cecilia, about how hard she worked and how she never got to do what she wanted to do. Then I heard the cops had arrested a guy and I got scared all over again. What if the guy they caught tried to lay it off on me — you know, I saw this girl,

I bet *she* took the box? So I waited. Nothing happened. I didn't hear anything about someone seeing me in the store — until you showed up. So I figured I'd be okay. I could use the money to do what Cecilia wanted."

"You keep saying that," Rebecca said. "What are you talking about?"

"Shopping," I said. "She's talking about shopping. You're going to send the stuff you bought to Mrs. Lee's sisters, aren't you?"

Amanda looked at me like maybe I wasn't a complete idiot.

"When Mr. Lee died, I figured I was in the clear for sure."

"But what about the guys who did it? Didn't you want them to get caught?"

"Sure," she said. "But I didn't want to be the one to ID them. The cops would ask me how I knew and what I was doing there, and that could open up a whole can of worms. I can just imagine how their lawyers would make me look. Besides, the cops already arrested one of them. I figured he would eventually cave and give up the other two."

"But the person they arrested is my friend," I reminded her. "How could he cave? You said yourself how surprised he looked. He doesn't know who those guys are."

I noticed then that Rebecca was frowning at Amanda, but in a different way now, not in the way she had been before when she was making it clear that she didn't like Amanda. No, this was different.

"What's the matter?" I said.

Rebecca looked across the table at Amanda, who had a different look on her face now, too.

"When we caught up with you, you said we were making a big mistake. What did you mean?" Rebecca said.

Amanda leaned back in the booth, looking at Rebecca now like she was more than an airhead preppy. Then she turned to me. What was going on?

"You said you wanted to clear your friend, right?" Amanda said.

"We just did," I said. "You said he came into the store *before* those other two guys. That's exactly what Vin told me and what he told the police. He said he just went into the store to buy himself a Coke. You said he came in and went to the cooler where the pop is kept. Vin said he was stunned when he saw one of the guys holding a gun. You said the same thing — that he seemed really surprised when he saw the gun. He said he turned around and saw the guys with the gun. He said he couldn't believe it. He said after the shooting, he was practically in shock. You said that's what it looked like, like he was in shock. He says that's why he ran. He wasn't thinking. He was scared. He said you could tell the police exactly what you just told me, and it would prove that he didn't have anything to do with it. He was just in the wrong place at the wrong time."

Amanda stared at me for a few seconds. Then she said, "If he came into the store to buy himself a can of Coke, and if he didn't know those two guys, how come your friend took *three* cans of Coke out of the cooler instead of just one?"

CHAPTER SIXTEEN

What I wanted to do was give her back her lock box and tell her to get out of there. Tell her to send the stuff she'd bought to Cecilia Lee's sisters so that at least one good thing would come out of the whole mess. And let Vin take his chances with what they already had on him. Let him rot, for all I cared.

What I did when I was finally breathing normally again was ask Rebecca if I could borrow her cell phone.

"You calling the cops on me?" Amanda said.

"Not yet," I said. I called Riel. He said he'd just got home. I told him where I was and asked him if he could come over. I guess he must have picked up on something in my voice because he sounded concerned when he said, "What's going on, Mike?"

I said I'd tell him when he got here. I said, "It's important."

"I'll be there in five minutes," he said. Just like that, no more questions. That, right there, was why I was glad I lived where I did and why it mostly didn't bother me that he was on my case all the time about homework and chores.

Five minutes later, he walked into the restaurant. He spotted me right away. He said hi to Rebecca when he got to the booth. He looked at Amanda — at her short blond hair and the little scar near her eyebrow from where her piercing was. Then he looked at me.

"This is Amanda Brown," I said. "She's the girl Vin saw in the store."

Amanda just nodded. Something had changed in how she was acting. If you ask me, she was a little ashamed.

Riel sat down in the booth next to Rebecca, who scooched over so that she was sitting as far away from him as she could. She was really going to have to learn to relax around him.

Amanda repeated her whole story. Riel didn't interrupt her, not even when she got to the part about the Cokes, not even when she said, "He was surprised all right. I don't think he knew what was going to happen. But you know something? When those guys ran out, he looked at the Cokes in his hand and before he ran, he put them back in the cooler."

When she had finished, Riel said, "Can you describe the guys who did it?"

She nodded.

"And you'd recognize them again if you saw them?"

"Yeah."

Riel looked at me. "You know what this means about Vin, right, Mike?"

Boy, did I ever.

Riel turned back to Amanda. "If you tell them everything you told me, and if you describe the guys or can help the police identify them, and if you tell them that you know what you did was wrong and that you'll return the money — "

"I already spent most of it on stuff for Cecilia's sisters."

Riel seemed to understand about that. "If you tell the police everything you told me and say that you know what you did was wrong and that you're willing to make restitution, they might not go too hard on you. But you are going to have to tell them. You want the guys who shot Mrs. Lee to be held to account, don't you? You don't want them to get away with it, right? Not if she was your friend."

"I'll tell them," Amanda said. I think she had made up her mind even before I called Riel. Anyway, she didn't have much choice now.

Riel asked Amanda how old she was. She said sixteen. He asked her if she wanted one of her parents to come to the police station with her. Amanda shook her head.

"My mom's dead. And my dad wouldn't be much help. I'm okay. I can handle it."

Riel told her she could ask for a lawyer. He told her how she should do it. He offered to stay with her, but she said again that she could handle it. Finally he paid for our drinks and we all got into his car so he could drive us to the police station, where Amanda told her story for the third time.

* * *

The following Wednesday night when I got home from work, Riel and Susan were sitting on the couch. Susan had her wedding binder open in her lap and was talking about flowers. I could tell Riel wasn't listening. He had one eye on the TV, which was tuned to a news channel. He always watched the news. I wondered if Susan was going to get annoyed with him again. When they got to the local stuff, they said that the police had made an arrest in the robbery and shooting at the convenience store, and they showed photographs of the two guys they had arrested. They were both older than Vin, both eighteen, so there was no problem about naming them and showing their faces. The pictures were only on for a few seconds, but that's all I needed. One of those faces burned itself into my brain. But before I could say anything, the phone rang.

"You want to get that, Mike?" Riel said. I could see why he didn't want to get up. He had his arm around Susan now and she looked like she was snuggled in there nice and close.

I picked up the phone in the kitchen. It was Rebecca.

"I was just watching the news," she said. She was breathing fast, like she was out of breath.

"Me, too."

"Did you see those guys, the ones they arrested?"

"Yeah."

"I recognized one of them, Mike. From the video store."

"Me, too," I said. "The guy they called Shane." The guy with the mostly shaved head. "He came into that first video store we went to. He was watching you when you were talking to that first clerk."

"He was?" Rebecca said. She sounded surprised.

"Isn't that what you mean, Rebecca?"

"No. I meant the *other* guy. What was his name again?"

"They said his name was Richard."

"Richard was in the video store where Amanda worked. He came out when we were talking to that clerk at the second store, the one who gave us Amanda's phone number. He was with another guy. They both took off when the cop car showed up. You didn't notice?" I remembered the two guys, but I hadn't looked at them that closely. "And you're saying the other one was in the first video store? You think that's just a coincidence, Mike?"

I didn't.

We talked a little longer — it was mostly me, telling her not to worry, the guys had been arrested, there was nothing they could do to us.

I'd just finished talking to Rebecca when the phone rang again. This time it was Vin's mom. Right after that, the phone rang a third time.

"It's for you," I said, handing the phone to Riel. It was a woman. I wondered if it was Kate.

Riel's whole face changed as he listened to what she said. But he didn't say anything when he hung up. He just sat down again beside Susan, who had moved on now to table decorations. I could tell Riel wasn't listening, but I wasn't sure if Susan noticed.

* * *

Riel was in the kitchen when I came downstairs the next morning. He glanced at me as he stuffed papers into his briefcase.

"I have to run, Mike. You can get your breakfast

and get to school on time, right?"

I glanced at the clock on the stove.

"It's early," I said.

"I have to make a stop on the way to school."

"What about Susan? Is she still sleeping?"

"She's at home. She didn't stay over last night."

"Oh."

Riel paused to look at me.

"Mike, there's something I need to talk to you about. Why don't you meet me after school? We'll go out, maybe grab a bite to eat, okay?"

I got a bad feeling.

"I can't," I said. "They let Vin out. I want to go over to his place to see him."

Riel didn't look happy at that. "You think that's a good idea?" he said.

"I have to talk to him," I said. "There's something I have to ask him."

Riel looked at me for a few moments. Then he said, "Okay." He glanced at his watch. "I guess it can keep."

* * *

When I took my seat in French class, I glanced over two rows at Imogen. Right away she looked down at her desk and didn't look up again. As soon as class was over, she grabbed her books and almost ran for the door. I chased after her.

"Hey, Imogen," I said. She was up ahead of me in the hall. Either she didn't hear me or she was pretending she didn't. I walked faster. "Imogen." I grabbed her arm and she spun around. Her cheeks were red and she didn't want to look at me. "I just want to know how Sal is," I said.

I had called his aunt's place half a dozen times over the past few days, but every time I did, his mother said he couldn't come to the phone. I even stopped by once. His mother had looked surprised when she answered the door. She told me that Sal was sleeping, but that she would be sure to tell him that I'd been by. But her eyes kept skipping away from me, which gave me the idea that she wasn't telling the truth, and that the truth was that Sal didn't want to see me or talk to me. She told me he should be back at school soon.

"How's he doing?" I said to Imogen.

She didn't tell me to get lost. She didn't tell me that it was none of my business. She didn't say anything at all. She just burst into tears. I was so surprised that I let go of her arm, and she ran into the girls' bathroom.

"I guess you didn't hear the news," Rebecca said when I told her what had happened.

"News? What news? Sal is okay, isn't he?"

"Sal and Imogen broke up," Rebecca said. "Imogen's been crying in the girls' bathroom for two days now."

That was news to me.

"What happened?" I said.

Rebecca just shrugged. "Imogen just said Sal dumped her. She didn't say why — not that I heard of, anyway."

"Oh."

* * *

When I pushed the doorbell at Vin's house after school, Vin's mother answered the door. She said Vin had just gone to the store to get some milk. She said he had volunteered to do it, even though she used to have to badger him in the past when she wanted him to do an errand. She said she thought that was because he had been locked up for a while and now he couldn't stand to be inside. She said he should be back in a minute and invited me in. While we waited, she talked to me.

"His lawyer says there's a good chance they'll drop most of the charges," she said. "They believe him now that he didn't have anything to do with the actual robbery or shooting, thanks to you finding that girl. He had some of the stolen money on him and he knew it was stolen, so they're saying they could charge him for that and maybe even with being an accessory after the fact. But it was only ten or fifteen dollars. And his lawyer thinks that, given what the police already know about the two people who did it, Vin can make a good case that he *was* scared to tell the truth — and he was scared, Mike. You've seen him. You know. That's why he didn't do the right thing." She glanced at me. "Vin told me you were the only one who believed him. I can't thank you enough."

Vin came through the front door carrying a jug of milk, which he handed to his mother. He looked a lot better this time. He said it was great to be home again. Then he thanked me.

Right.

His mother smiled at the two of us. Then she said, "Well, I'll leave you two alone to talk."

We went into the living room. I waited until Vin's mother had gone upstairs. Then I said, "You lied to me, Vin."

"I said I had nothing to do with it, and I didn't," Vin said. "You heard what that girl said. She said I looked more surprised than she did. And the reason for that, Mike, is that I didn't know."

"But you knew who the guys were. You knew the whole time. You could have identified them."

He didn't deny it. "One of them, Shane — not the guy who did the shooting but the other one — he's friends with this guy I met from when I was in custody. I ran into them earlier that day. They were going to shoot some pool and they asked me if I wanted to go with them. I didn't have anything better to do, so I said sure. Afterward they wanted something to drink, some Cokes, so I volunteered to get them. They pulled over at this store they said they knew and I went in. That's the only reason I went in. I was surprised when they came in after me. Turns out they pulled the car around behind the store just after I went in. They were thinking about robbing the place before they even came in. But I didn't know. I'm not kidding you, Mike, no one was more surprised than me when they did what they did. Turns out that they'd heard the old guy kept a lot of money around. They were mad when the woman didn't hand over more than she did."

"You shouldn't have run, Vin. You should have stayed and called the cops."

Vin shook his head. "You don't know these guys, Mike. They know lots of people. If I'd ratted them out, they would have got me for sure. Look what they did to Sal. There was no way I wanted to be the one to tell the cops who they were. Thanks to you, I didn't have to. The girl's the one who ID'd them. Not me."

"You knew the girl saw them, didn't you?"

"I saw her face in that mirror. She was looking right at them."

"Did you tell them that?"

He looked down at the coffee table. Boy, it's never a good sign when people look down instead of right at you when they're talking to you.

"I was scared, Mike," he said. "After we got out of there, I was really jazzing, you know? I told them someone saw us run out of the store. I said the person who saw us could probably identify me for sure. I said, there was a girl in there, too. She saw everything." He shook his head. "They really freaked out. That's when I realized that if the girl went to the cops, it could be good for me. She could say I wasn't involved." He looked at me. "She's some sharp girl, noticing those three Cokes with everything else that was happening."

"She says you put them back in the cooler."

He shrugged. "I have a record, Mike. They've got my prints. I thought if I put them back . . . "

Right.

"Anyway, there I was, hoping the girl would show up so she could back me up when I said I had nothing to do with it. And there they were, hoping she wouldn't show up because maybe she could identify them. Then nothing happened. The girl didn't go to the cops."

"But somehow they knew *I* was looking for her."

Vin's eyes met mine. "I know. There was a guy in there, Mike, that I shouldn't have talked to, but I did. I was going crazy, you know, worrying about what was going to happen to me. I couldn't talk to any of the staff — they write everything down. I couldn't talk to my mother. So I talked to this guy who, it turns out, knows someone who knows the guy who had the gun. I didn't know that, Mike. I swear I didn't. I told him I was scared because someone had identified me. I told him you were my only chance."

"You told this guy I was looking for the girl?"

He nodded. "I guess he passed it along, Mike. I'm sorry. But no harm done, right?"

"They followed us, Vin. They followed Rebecca and me. Because you told them we were looking for the girl."

"Yeah," Vin said. "But I didn't tell them that you found her."

"You didn't know that until she went to the cops."

"Yeah, I did," Vin said. He grinned at me. "You never were a good liar, Mike. The last time you came to see me, when I asked you if you'd found the girl and you said no, I knew you were lying. But I didn't tell anyone that. I told them what you told me. I told them that you struck out."

He made it sound like that made him some kind of hero, when the truth was that if he'd passed the word along to his friends and if they had got to Amanda . . . I shuddered when I remembered what they had done to Sal. If they'd done the same thing to Amanda, she never would have agreed to go to the cops. For sure she would never have agreed to identify them. I was having trouble breathing all of a sudden. I wanted to get out of there. But before I left, I had to know one more thing.

"How did they know where Sal lives?" I said.

"I already told you, Mike. I don't know." He looked me right in the eye when he said it. "When I told them someone saw us run out of the store and that I was pretty sure he could identify me, they asked me if I knew who it was. I said I thought it was some guy who used to go to the same school as me way back when. But I didn't tell them his name, I swear it. Geeze, Mike, do you really think I'd fix it so those guys would go after Sal? I know these guys, Mike. I know what they'd do."

"You didn't tell them where he moved to?"

"What?" I don't believe I'd ever seen Vin look so surprised. "When did he move?"

"A few months back. His mother had to sell the house on account of his dad being sick. They had to move."

"No kidding. You'd have thought my mom would have mentioned it." Vin's house was on the next street over from Sal's old house. You could see the house from Vin's bedroom window. "His old man's not doing so well then, huh?"

"No," I said. "He's not."

Vin shook his head. "I didn't tell them anything about Sal. I didn't even tell them his name. I swear it."

On his face, I saw sincerity. But what I saw on Vin's face and what was in his heart didn't always match up the way they used to when we were kids.

I started to get up. "Hey, Vin, what if I hadn't found the girl and found a way to get her to tell the truth? What were you going to do?"

"I don't know," he said. "I was trying not to think about that. I was counting on you. You really came through for me."

"Yeah," I said. "I gotta go, Vin."

"Yeah. Sure. Hey, Mike, wish me luck, huh?"

CHAPTER SEVENTEEN

Riel was waiting for me when I got home.

So was Sal. They were in the kitchen together.

Riel got up from the table when I came in. He said, "I have some test papers to mark." He glanced at me as he went into the other room.

I sat down at the table opposite Sal.

"I've been calling you," I said.

He nodded, but didn't apologize for not taking my calls and not calling me back.

"How are you feeling?" I said.

"I went back to work last night. I'll be back at school on Monday." He looked at me. "There was a picture in the paper a couple of days ago, Mike. Did you see it? It was a picture of those two guys that got arrested for the shooting."

"I saw them on TV."

"The thing is," Sal said, "I recognized one of the guys."

"What?"

"Not from the store," Sal said. "After I heard the shots, I saw the two guys running down the alley. One of them glanced back over his shoulder — I remember now that I saw him turn. But by then Vin was coming out of the store. I focused on Vin, you know? But that guy, he must have remembered me because . . . " He looked up at me. "The night I got beat up, I'd been at work."

"Yeah?"

"It was really busy that night, but there were only two registers open. Mine was one of them. Anyway, I was pushing through orders and I was hardly even looking at the customers. Then this guy ordered a couple of our extra value meals. You have to ask, Is that for here or to go? — you know, so you can either put the food on a tray or bag it for takeout. He said it was for here and, I don't know, I looked up at him and, pop, his eyes went real wide, you know, like he was surprised. I didn't think about it at the time. We get all kinds of people in there, Mike. And late at night, some of them have been partying or whatever. You never know."

He shifted in his chair. His face was a papery colour and seemed tight, like he was holding something back. I wondered if he was on painkillers.

"Anyway, this guy looked at me. He looked surprised. He paid for the food, but he said he'd changed his mind, he wanted his stuff bagged for takeout. So, big deal, right? People change their minds all the time. I bagged his stuff and he left. I didn't watch him or anything — I had a whole line of customers. But I noticed he was with another guy."

I wanted to tell him to say it, just say it. But this was Sal. Sal took his time with things.

"Then I opened the paper the other day and I saw pictures of the two guys who robbed that store. And you know what, Mike? One of them was the guy who came into the restaurant the night I was beat up."

Sal was the only person I knew who actually referred to his workplace as a restaurant. Maybe they'd pounded it into his head, the way they made everyone at the video store say, How may I help you? before they said anything else.

"I'm pretty sure now that he recognized me from the day of the robbery. That's why he looked so surprised. And I think maybe the fact that I looked up at him the way I did when I hadn't looked at anyone else who was in line ahead of him, I think maybe that made him worry that I'd seen something at the convenience store, you know, that maybe I was putting two and two together and was going to call the cops on him."

It took a moment for me to get it.

"Those were the guys who beat you up?"

"They were the guys the cops arrested. And they were in the restaurant the night I got beat up. I've been thinking, Mike. What could have happened is they could have followed me home. When I got to the building where my aunt lives, I remembered that I had finished all the milk before I went to work. So I went across the street to buy some. And when I got back to the building, they jumped me. So what could have happened — " He looked down for a moment and then back up into my eyes. "I thought they must have been waiting for me when I got home. And I figured the only way that could have happened is that you told Vin where I had moved to. But now I figure what happened is that they followed me and waited while I went into the store, and then they jumped me. They didn't already know where I live. They followed me. Which means that I was wrong when I accused you of telling Vin where I live. So I'm sorry about that."

He was still looking at me and I could tell he was sorry. But there was something else.

"Well, at the time you said it, it was the only thing that made sense to you." I'm pretty sure I wouldn't have been so quick to jump to the same conclusion if our places had been reversed. But he was apologizing. And he was my friend. And in the past week, I had realized how much things had changed between us and how I didn't like that. I wanted things to be back to the way they used to be. "It's okay," I said. "So we're good then?" I smiled at him. "Still friends?"

He didn't smile back.

"There's something else, Mike," he said. He took in a deep breath and then winced. I guess he still hurt from the beating the two guys had given him. "I was pretty mad. I told Imogen that the only way those guys could have found me was if you told Vin. I — " He shook his head. "I told her you were so tight with Vin, maybe you were even in on it with him."

I stared at him. Boy, he hadn't thought much of me.

Sal has big black eyes that sparkle when he's clowning around but that can look sad too. They looked sad now.

"Imogen told me what she did, Mike. She wanted to get even with you for what you did — for what she thought you did. So she called the cops on you."

Wait a minute . . .

"She didn't tell me she was going to do it. She didn't tell me until a couple of days ago. I'm sorry, Mike. If I'd known — "

"*Imogen* called Crime Stoppers on me?"

Sal nodded. "I'm not going out with her anymore, Mike. I told her we're through."

I guess that explained all her tears.

"I was wrong to say what I did to Imogen. I was wrong to accuse you of something you didn't do," Sal said. "But Mike? I wasn't wrong about Vin. Maybe he didn't pull the trigger, but he didn't try to stop it, either. And he lied to the cops. He tried to protect those guys."

"He was scared, Sal. He thought those guys were going to — "

"*He* was scared?" Sal's whole face changed. It got red. "My mom was scared, Mike. She thought if I kept doing what I was doing, which is telling the truth, someone was going to kill me. For telling the truth, Mike. *I* was scared. I was scared she was right. You know what it's like to be beat up like that, Mike? You know what goes through your head when two big guys jump you and start pounding on you and you don't know what's going on — it comes into your head, Mike, that maybe they're trying to kill you. Or, even if they aren't, that they're going to kick too hard or they're going to try to use your head as a football and you're going to end up a vegetable. That's what you think about, Mike. You lie there on the ground and you try to curl up and you cover your head with your arms as best you can and you pray they don't do any permanent damage."

Geeze.

"I'm sorry, Sal."

"You know what, Mike? I don't care if Vin was scared. If you ask me, he had a right to be, hanging out with guys like that. But that was his choice. He decided to hang with those guys. He decided to keep his mouth shut instead of telling the truth. He watched them do what they did and then he pretended he was just an innocent bystander, he didn't know anything, he didn't know those guys. But that wasn't true. It wasn't true at all, Mike."

Boy, he was yelling the words at me now.

"Hey, Sal, I didn't know that."

Sal didn't say anything for a few seconds. "I'm not mad at you, Mike," he said finally. "But Vin?" He shook his head. "I don't care if I never see him again, you know?"

I nodded.

Sal winced again as he got to his feet.

"I gotta go," he said. "I fell behind in school. I have to catch up."

"You want to borrow some of my notes?" I said. It was all I had to offer.

He smiled. For the first time in a long time, my friend Sal smiled at me.

"I'm shooting for A's this year, Mike," he said. "And so far I'm doing pretty well. So if you don't mind, I'm going to take Rebecca up on *her* offer."

"Rebecca?"

"Yeah. She said she'd lend me her notes. Plus, I can actually read her writing. See you at school on Monday, okay, Mike?"

I said okay. The truth was, I was looking forward to it.

* * *

Riel came into the kitchen after Sal had left.

"So," he said, "everything's back to normal?"

"Sort of, I guess."

Riel sat down where Sal had been sitting just a minute before.

"Mike, there's something I have to talk to you about."

Oh-oh. Here it came.

"It's about Kate, right?" I said.

Riel looked surprised.

"How do you know about Kate?" he said.

I just shrugged.

"Is Susan upset?" I said.

"Upset?"

"You know, because you changed your mind."

"Susan supports my decision," Riel said. "I just want to make sure you're going to be okay with it."

I didn't know what to say. "I like Susan," I said slowly.

"I know you do. And there are going to be a lot of changes around here, what with the wedding and Susan moving in and her crazy schedule and now mine is going to be even crazier."

I stared at him.

"What are you talking about?" I said. "I thought you were getting back with Kate. I thought you and Susan — "

The look he gave me made me nervous.

"I heard you talking to Dave Jones one day after school," I said, embarrassed to be admitting to eavesdropping. "It sounded like you were going to break up with Susan, only she didn't know it yet. Then someone named Kate called you one night and you left the house right away. I thought you were going to meet her."

He looked at me a little longer, probably to make a point about listening in on other people's conversations. Then he said, "You've got it wrong, Mike. I'm not breaking up with Susan. I'm going back to my old job. And when you've been away as long as I have, they make you jump through a lot of hoops first. In my case, they wanted to make sure I was making the right decision." He meant because he had been shot that time. "I wanted to make sure, too. So I had a few talks with Kate. She works for the police, in human resources. I talked to other people, too. I had to."

"That's where you were when you were supposed to be trying out wedding menus, right?" I said.

He nodded. "Susan and I had a long talk that night. She's okay with it, Mike. As for that night when I went to see Kate . . . Kate really helped me, Mike. She arranged everything. She's also an old friend, so I told her if there was ever anything I could do for her, all she had to do was ask."

Oh.

"She asked, huh?" I said.

"Yeah," Riel said. "The carpet she waited six months for finally arrived. She had to move all the furniture out of her living room and dining room that night so that the installers could put the carpet in first thing the next morning. I helped her."

"So you and Susan are still getting married?"

"Of course we are. I love Susan, Mike."

"But you're going to be a cop — police officer — not a teacher?"

"Yeah. You okay with that?"

"I guess so." If it was what he wanted. "Sure."

"My hours are going to be a whole lot less regular."

"I'm going to be sixteen soon," I said. "I'll be fine."

"You sure? Because — "

"I'll be fine," I said again. But, boy, it felt good that he cared enough to ask.

"There one's more thing," he said. I braced myself. "We have to go downtown tomorrow after school. To try on tuxedos. Susan wants to cross that off her list."

Which reminded me. "Susan said I'm in the wedding party, but she didn't say as what. You want me to be an usher or something?"

"I'm sorry, Mike. With everything else that was going on, I forgot to ask you. I was hoping you'd be groomsman."

"What's that?"

"It's an attendant to the groom. Dave's going to be best man." He meant Dave Jones, who was his best friend. "You have to be at least eighteen for that job, so he more than fits the bill. But I want you up there with Susan and me when we get married. How about it?"

I told him I'd be honoured.

And I meant it.

The Chloe and Levesque Mysteries

Over the Edge
Can Chloe figure out who pushed
Adam over the edge?
Red Maple and White Pine
Shortlist
$6.99   0-439-95632-3

Double Cross
Finding out what
happened to Jonah's mother leads
Chloe straight into danger!
$6.99   0-439-95634-X

Scared to Death
What — or *who* — has scared
Tessa to death?
Arthur Ellis Award
$6.99   0-439-95633-1

Break and Enter
Someone is setting Chloe up . . .
Arthur Ellis Award
$6.99   0-439-95635-8

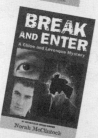

No Escape

Nobody but Chloe will give Caleb
the benefit of the doubt . . .
White Pine and Manitoba Young
Reader's Choice Shortlist
$6.99   0-439-95636-6

Not a Trace

Everyone assumes David Mitchell
is the killer . . . Everyone except
Chloe.
Arthur Ellis Award Nominee
$6.99   0-439-95760-5

Body, Crime, Suspect:
How a Murder
Investigation
Really Works

Go behind the scenes of
a crime case and see how
it's solved.
Arthur Ellis and Red
Cedar Award Shortlist
$5.99   0-439-98769-5

The Mike and Riel Mysteries

Hit and Run

Was the hit and run
accident that killed Mike's
mother *really* an accident?
Red Maple Award
$6.99   0-439-97418-6

Truth and Lies

One little lie leads to
another, and ends up
making Mike the lead
suspect in a *murder*
investigation . . .
$6.99   0-439-96919-0

Dead and Gone

The discovery of a long-buried body
rekindles a murder
investigation that had been
unsolved for years . . .
Red Maple Honour Book
$7.99   0-439-96759-7

Seeing and Believing

If Mike believes one of his best
friends . . . he might lose the other.
$7.99   0-439-94608-5

The Robyn Hunter Mysteries

Last Chance
Can Robyn trust Nick
enough to give him one
last chance . . . ?
$8.99   0-439-95229-8

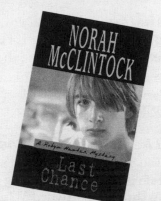

You Can Run
Robyn and Nick have to find
Trisha before she disappears
for good . . .
$8.99   0-439-95230-1

Other Titles

Mistaken Identity

If Zanny's own father isn't who
she thought he was . . . then who
is *she*?
Arthur Ellis Award
$5.99   0-590-24627-5

The Body in the Basement

The body found in Tasha's parents'
café is only the beginning . . .
Arthur Ellis Award Winner, Red
Maple Award First Runner-Up
and Manitoba Young Reader's
Choice Award Shortlist
$5.99   0-590-24983-5

Sins of the Father

What does Mick have to do
to clear his father's name?
Arthur Ellis Award Winner
and Red Maple Award Shortlist
$5.99   0-590-12488-9

Password: Murder

Could the clues that Harley discovers
mean that his father's death wasn't
really his fault?
Red Maple Award Shortlist
$6.99   0-439-94764-2